No one should die a virgin.

Shane took two steps into the bedroom from the ensuite bath and stalled.

Mary Jane lay snuggled beneath the covers of his bed. She didn't say a word. She didn't have to. The invitation was obvious. His body tightened at the idea.

He crossed the room and sat down on the edge of the bed. "This isn't a good idea." The fact that save for the towel he was naked and that she also appeared to be wasn't helping.

"You might be right," she allowed. "But it's my idea and I don't want to wake up tomorrow wishing I'd had the courage to do what I'd really wanted to...."

DEBRA WEBB

COLBY
REBUILT

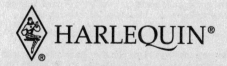

HARLEQUIN®

TORONTO • NEW YORK • LONDON
AMSTERDAM • PARIS • SYDNEY • HAMBURG
STOCKHOLM • ATHENS • TOKYO • MILAN • MADRID
PRAGUE • WARSAW • BUDAPEST • AUCKLAND

To the fans.

ISBN-13: 978-0-373-69290-3
ISBN-10:   0-373-69290-0

COLBY REBUILT

ABOUT THE AUTHOR

Debra Webb was born in Scottsboro, Alabama, to parents who taught her that anything is possible if you want it bad enough. She began writing at age nine. Eventually, she met and married the man of her dreams, and she tried various occupations, including selling vacuum cleaners and working in a factory, a daycare center, a hospital and a department store. When her husband joined the military, they moved to Berlin, Germany, and Debra became a secretary in the commanding general's office. By 1985 they were back in the States and finally moved to Tennessee, to a small town where everyone knows everyone else. With the support of her husband and two beautiful daughters, Debra took up writing again, looking to mystery and movies for inspiration. In 1998 her dream of writing for Harlequin Books came true. You can write to Debra with your comments at P.O. Box 64, Huntland, Tennessee 37345 or visit her Web site at www.debrawebb.com to find out exciting news about her next book.

Books by Debra Webb

HARLEQUIN INTRIGUE

*Colby Agency
†The Equalizers

CAST OF CHARACTERS

Shane Allen—Former U.S. marshal turned Colby Agency investigator. Nothing will stop Shane from getting the job done.

Mary Jane Brooks—Mary Jane will do whatever it takes to solve her sister's murder.

Victoria Colby-Camp—The head of the Colby Agency. Victoria will see that the mystery of the remains discovered in the rubble of the agency's former home is solved.

Rebecca Brooks—Her remains have been found nearly one year after her murder.

Detective Brandon Bailen—One of Chicago P.D.'s finest. He has been working the Brooks case since the beginning.

Anthony Chambers—The CEO of Horizon Software, the man Rebecca Brooks was set to testify against.

Jason Mackey—Musician and cousin to Anthony Chambers.

Special Agent John LeMire—The FBI agent assigned to the Brooks case.

U.S. Marshal Derrick Mitchell—The U.S. marshal assigned to the Brooks case. Shane's former partner and the reason Shane and his wife divorced.

Jose Torres—Jason Mackey's best friend.

Teresa Thomas—Jason Mackey's girlfriend.

Ann Martin—Colby Agency investigator.

Chapter One

Mary Jane Brooks understood the news was bad the moment she opened her door and saw the resigned slump of the detective's shoulders.

"We've confirmed that the—" Detective Brandon Bailen, Chicago PD, cleared his throat "—the remains are Rebecca's."

Mary Jane's heart plummeted and her knees weakened. Holding on to the doorframe was all that kept her vertical. "You're certain there's no mistake." She moistened her trembling lips and struggled to hold back the tears. "Labs do make mistakes. I read about—"

"There's no mistake, Ms. Brooks."

Rebecca was dead.

On some level Mary Jane had known for a while now that her sister was *gone*, but hearing the words somehow made it new…made it hurt so badly.

"Thank you, Detective." Mary Jane managed to draw in a deep, shuddering breath. "Do you know what happened? Was she—" working up the courage to say the word took monumental effort *"—murdered?"*

Sympathy softened Bailen's usually firm expression. He was a tall, thin man with stark features, yet he was the kindest cop she had met during this awful ordeal. "Yes, ma'am, we have reason to believe so."

Mary Jane closed her eyes. She wasn't sure she wanted to hear the details, but how else could she ever know the whole truth? She opened her eyes and looked directly into the detective's. "How?"

"Massive head trauma."

The image of a broken and battered skull flashed in her mind. She tightened her hold on the doorframe, her fingers ice cold. "I see."

But she didn't see. Her sister hadn't been in trouble. She had been guilty of nothing more than doing the right thing. Rebecca had told her weeks before she disappeared that she was going to have to take a stand against her employer. She hadn't elaborated on the specifics, only that the company or the CEO or maybe both were up to something illegal. Rebecca had known she had to do something…the right thing.

Mary Jane had known the situation was far more serious than her sister had related when the federal authorities—FBI as well as the Marshals Service— had called to inquire as to Rebecca's whereabouts less than forty-eight hours after she had vanished.

Now, eleven months later, Mary Jane's worst fears were confirmed.

There was nothing she could do but bury her only sibling just as she had buried both her parents in the past three months.

Mary Jane was alone. The realization crashed in around her, leaving her shaking in spite of her best efforts to remain stoic.

Her whole family was gone.

"When can I claim her remains?" Mary Jane forced the question past her lips. Seeing that Rebecca had a proper service and burial was the one remaining detail she could attend to for her sister. In all these months one would think that she would have been better prepared for this moment. But she wasn't. It felt impossible…surreal.

"That may take some time," Bailen warned, his tone careful. "The FBI is launching a new investigation and, of course, we'll be coordinating our own with theirs in an effort to get to the bottom of what really happened."

Mary Jane understood. "You'll keep me posted?" That seemed like the proper question to ask next in light of the circumstances. She had no idea how this sort of business was handled. Her only experience with criminal investigations was watching television. Surely the authorities kept the family informed.

Dear God. Her sister was dead.

Mary Jane was alone.

"As soon as we know any details," Bailen promised, "I'll pass along what I can."

Her head moved up and down in a motion of agreement, but Mary Jane's thoughts were churning on the horror evolving in her head. Rebecca running away from her killer...or maybe struggling with him. Him bashing her over the head...once, twice and then again.

"Where?" Mary Jane hadn't even realized the inquiry had taken shape in her brain until she heard the word echo in the corridor outside her apartment. She should have asked the detective in, she realized belatedly. Instead, she'd stood here in the doorway and listened to the news no one ever wanted to hear.

Bailen looked confused. "Where?"

"Where did you find her...remains?"

With that question, the full implications collapsed around her with new, brutal impact. She had another funeral to plan. It seemed unbelievable. So much death in so little time.

"That's part of the puzzle," Bailen said wearily. "Her remains were found amid the rubble of the building downtown that once housed the Colby Agency."

Colby Agency?

"What sort of business is that?" Mary Jane wasn't familiar with the name. Insurance? Staffing?

"The Colby Agency is a private investigation

agency," Bailen explained. "Been a prominent Chicago fixture for more than a quarter of a century. The building was blown up last Christmas Eve by thugs attempting to cover up fraud at an investment firm located at the same address. For a while there was some question as to whether the Colby Agency or the investment firm was the target, but that investigation is closed now."

"Why would my sister have been at a private investigation agency?" That didn't make sense to Mary Jane. Why wouldn't Rebecca have told her about that kind of thing? But then, she hadn't told her everything about the trouble with her employer. Did the Colby Agency have something to do with her testimony against Horizon Software?

There was no way for Rebecca to even guess. Her sister would have kept things from her in an effort to protect her. It was part of the "older sibling" mentality. She hadn't told Mary Jane the gritty truth about her employer for that very reason. Sure Mary Jane had known there were problems and that Rebecca was going to blow the whistle, but, as Mary Jane had learned over the past few months, those details had only scratched the surface. Mary Jane doubted she would ever know everything that had happened between her sister, Horizon Software and the federal authorities.

"I can't answer that question, Ms. Brooks," the detective admitted, drawing her from her painful thoughts. "But I can tell you that we're going to find out. That's a promise."

Mary Jane thanked the detective and then watched him go. The thought of going back into her apartment was almost unbearable. She knew what would happen.

She would go inside and close the door. And then she would break down. The idea of being in public, if only in the deserted corridor of her apartment building, helped to keep her unsteady composure in place. She had to be the strong one when it came to situations like this. She'd always been the one everyone counted on to handle the routine things life threw in her path…the one who took care of things no one else had the time or inclination to. Rebecca had been too busy making her mark in the business world to bother with the everyday trivialities.

Now she was alone. Completely alone.

Mary Jane straightened away from the door, squared her shoulders in defiance of the trembling rampant in her body. Yes, she would cry. And then she would pull herself together and notify the distant relatives; and then she would make the memorial service arrangements—with or without the remains.

Then, when those necessary arrangements were out of the way, there was one other thing she decided she had to do.

She had to know for certain why Rebecca was dead.

Rebecca Brooks had been a good person. A wonderful woman, barely thirty-two, with her entire life ahead of her. She had gone to church most Sundays and had provided significant financial support for her elderly parents. Rebecca's help was the reason Mary Jane had been able to take an extended leave of absence from her teaching and stay home to care for their ailing parents rather than putting them in a nursing home.

Someone had murdered Rebecca for attempting to do the right thing—that had to be it, there simply was no other possible reason—and Mary Jane intended to see that whoever did this horrible thing was punished to the fullest extent of the law.

She had no idea how a murder investigation was conducted, but she did know where to start.

The Colby Agency.

The last place her sister had been before she was murdered. The place where she'd taken her final breath.

THE COLBY AGENCY HAD A NEW HOME. The tenth floor of a daring high-rise that gleamed against the Chicago skyline, displaying the same elegance and domination the world had come to expect of the prestigious agency.

Victoria Colby-Camp smiled as she looked out

over the city she loved. The view was somewhat different, but the pulse of the thriving metropolis stretching out before her was exactly the same. Thanksgiving was only a couple of weeks away, and Victoria had a great deal to be thankful for.

A soft rap on her door pulled Victoria's attention from her thoughts and the view. Ben Haygood, the agency's software and hardware expert, hovered at the door of her office.

"Yes, Ben?"

Now that, to his way of thinking, permission to enter had been granted, he burst into the room like the lean mass of vibrant energy he was. "Ma'am, we've encountered a slight glitch in the backup files we retrieved from the cyber storage system."

All had been lost in the explosion that had brought down the agency's former home. Ben had worked tirelessly for weeks since the opening of the new building to get everything in order. While working from their temporary quarters, minimal files had been pulled from cyber storage. Now that they were settled in their new home, hard copies of all electronically stored files were to be retrieved and reorganized.

"What sort of problem?" Victoria asked as she moved to the chair behind her desk. It wasn't the one she had used for so very many years—the one that James, her first husband and the founder of the Colby Agency had used—but it was quite comfortable and unquestionably elegant.

"The download has stopped midstream, and a secondary password has been requested." Ben pulled at the tie that already hung loosely at his throat. "I...ah...can't remember the secondary password we selected."

That didn't sound like Ben at all. He never forgot anything, much less a password. And even when there was a glitch, he generally took care of it and *then* told her about it. Evidently settling into the new building had disrupted his usually unshakable sangfroid. "Is that going to be a major problem?" she inquired cautiously, not wanting to make him more uncomfortable but needing clarification.

He shook his head enthusiastically. "I just need your authorization to override the password."

Now she got the picture. "Of course." Victoria settled into her chair and opened the laptop on her desk. "Walk me through the steps, Ben."

Ten seconds later Ben had his authorization.

"Thank you, ma'am."

Victoria gifted him with a smile she hoped relieved his obvious embarrassment. "Thank you, Ben, for taking such good care of our files."

He nodded as he backed out of her office, then he wheeled around and promptly bumped into Elaine Younger. Victoria smothered a laugh as Ben went overboard to offer his apologies. She sincerely hoped that one of these days he found someone who would truly appreciate him for all his many endearing assets. He could certainly do with a little grounding.

When Ben stepped aside, Elaine and Darla White, the agency's new receptionist, entered Victoria's office. Victoria didn't miss the way Ben stared, quite dreamily, after Darla before heading off to attend to the files. A secret smile tugged at the corners of Victoria's mouth. So maybe this was the reason Ben was so out of sorts lately. She would definitely have to look into the idea of a match between Ben and Darla.

"Do you have a moment, Victoria?"

"Certainly." Victoria indicated the chairs in front of her desk. "What can I do for you?"

Elaine gestured to the younger woman beside her and said, "I believe Darla is ready to take over on Monday, if that's agreeable."

Today was Friday the tenth, and Darla had worked a full two months under Elaine's tutelage to learn the ropes of being the receptionist for the Colby Agency, a job that entailed far more than merely answering the telephone and greeting visitors.

"You're absolutely right," Victoria concurred. "I've been very impressed with your progress, Darla."

The agency's newest employee blushed. Only twenty-two, this was Darla's first job since graduating college. Her father was a longtime friend, who owned one of Victoria's favorite restaurants. Victoria was more than glad to bring his lovely daughter on board. Darla, who wanted no part of the family business, made a fine addition to the agency's staff. In the past seven months, since getting business back up to full steam, they had gone through three trainees. Two had realized, within a week of starting, that the job was more then they could handle. The third, very promising candidate had been forced to leave after her fiancé had been reassigned to his company's Tokyo office.

Darla, however, had proven unshakable. She rolled with the punches and didn't let anything undermine her confidence. Now that Victoria thought about it, the nice young lady would be the perfect match for Ben.

"I'll be moving on to research..." Elaine went on, prodding Victoria back to the business at hand, "as soon as I'm back from my honeymoon."

More romance in bloom. A definite cause for celebration. Elaine and Brad Gibson were getting married next week. She would be working alongside her new husband in the agency's research group. This wasn't the first married couple to be employed by the Colby Agency. Nicole Reed and Ian Michaels had been successfully working together for years. In actuality the entire agency was like one big family. A feat that was a matter of pride to Victoria.

"Excellent." Victoria thought of her own husband, Lucas Camp, who was out of town yet again on business. She missed him when he was gone. Thankfully, he would be home this evening.

Mildred Ballard, Victoria's personal assistant and dear friend, stuck her head through the open doorway. "Detective Brandon Bailen is here to see you, Victoria."

"Thank you, Mildred. Tell Detective Bailen I'll be right with him." Victoria shifted her attention back to Elaine and Darla. "Why don't you take the rest of the day off, Elaine? Darla can manage without you, and I'm certain you have a million and one things to do."

Elaine's face lit up. "Thank you, Victoria."

The two hurried away and Victoria couldn't help feeling a bit nostalgic. Where had the years gone? She was a grandmother. Her son was happy with his lovely wife and beautiful baby girl. Another grandchild was on the way. Victoria sighed. Everything was changing, maybe a little too fast, but all for the good.

She rose as her visitor from the Chicago Police Department reached her door.

"Detective Bailen, this is an unexpected pleasure."

Bailen strode straight to Victoria's desk and took the hand she offered. "It's very good to see you, Victoria. The new place—" he glanced around her office "—is very elegant. It suits you."

"Thank you. We're still settling in." But she sensed this was not a social call, so she got straight down to business. "How may I help you this afternoon?"

"I have some rather belated and unsettling details from the lab regarding your former business address."

"Please—" Victoria gestured to a chair "—make yourself comfortable, Detective."

When Victoria had taken her seat, Bailen settled into his. From his weary expression she surmised that whatever he had come to report was not something he looked forward to passing along.

"We've just learned that the human remains discovered in the rubble of the Colby Agency building belonged to two different people."

His revelation sent a shock wave through Victoria. "Two? Was there another perpetrator involved that we didn't know about?" Elaine and Brad had barely survived that final night in the Colby Agency's former home. One of the perps who had tried to kill them had been murdered by his own people and left in the building. Additionally, the three musicians the agency had hired had been murdered in their van in the parking lot. But, so far as they knew, no one else had died inside the building except the one man. This revelation didn't quite add up.

Bailen's expression showed his own frustration. "According to the three convicted perps sitting in prison, there was only the four of them. The remains of their dead partner, as you know, were recovered a few weeks after the explosion."

Victoria didn't understand. "So, if there was no

one else in the building, how could there be remains from two people?"

"I wish I knew. All I can tell you is that there were two distinct sets of remains. Unfortunately, the second set of remains was separated from the first due to a simple human error, which caused the lab initially to report on only the one. Apparently, a recent inventory uncovered the glitch, and additional testing was done to confirm the error."

"You're certain—" Victoria hated to broach the idea but there was certainly just cause to be skeptical "—that the lab didn't make a mistake in where these particular remains came from?" After all, nearly a year had passed.

"We're certain," he assured her. "The trace evidence on the remains conclusively confirms where they were discovered."

"Do we have any idea who this person was?" The idea that remains were discovered in the rubble didn't guarantee that the individual had been in the building to visit the Colby Agency. A number of other businesses had been housed at that location, as well.

"Rebecca Brooks. Dental records confirmed her identity." Bailen seemed to consider the name before he continued. "We have reason to believe she was in the building to see someone in the Colby Agency. Part of the basis for that conclusion is related to several calls to your agency that showed up on the cellular records of her boyfriend. The calls were made during times that FBI surveillance puts the two of them together. But the primary rationale is that she was about to go into the Witness Security Program related to the Horizon Software case. We feel she may have felt the need for the kind of support you provide your clients."

Victoria was vaguely familiar with the Horizon Software case. Considering Ms. Brooks's situation prior to her death, Victoria could see how the detective had come to the conclusion that she had contacted the Colby Agency. Someone about to go into Witness Security wouldn't likely be making investments or purchasing insurance. None of the other businesses housed in the building that was the agency's former home would offer much to anyone in that position…except for the Colby Agency. Using her boyfriend's phone would certainly have provided some anonymity in her efforts to reach out under the circumstances.

Still, the conclusion was more hunch than fact. "I'd like the name of her boyfriend, if possible."

"Jason Mackey."

Recognition nudged Victoria. Jason Mackey was one of the musicians murdered in the parking lot only hours before the explosion. Victoria hadn't known him personally as she had the other two members of the trio. Mackey had been a last-minute stand-in with the group Mildred had hired to provide entertainment for the annual Colby Agency

Christmas party. The idea that Mackey wasn't a regular member of the band and that his girlfriend had been about to testify in a federal court case hardly seemed a chance occurrence, but wasn't totally outside the realm of possibility.

"Since no one at your agency," Bailen went on, "knew Jason Mackey or coordinated the entertainment for your office Christmas party directly with him, there's no apparent reason for him to have made those calls. On the other hand, Rebecca Brooks was in a prime position to be in search of exactly the sort of assistance your agency provides. Perhaps someone here spoke with her," he suggested, "maybe even met with her that day."

Speculation, sheer speculation. Or, as she had already considered, coincidence. Still, Victoria had never been one to believe in coincidences. The only question that remained was, What did the woman's death have to do with the Colby Agency?

Victoria needed an idea of where this was going. "Will you be heading an investigation, or is the Bureau going to handle this?" She was relatively certain the Bureau would have priority.

"I'll be coordinating with the Justice Department," Bailen confirmed her conclusion. "Both the Bureau and the Marshals have a vested interest in this case, though the Bureau will certainly be lead. I wanted to give you a heads-up. You could have information that would help us solve this mystery. If there is any record of her speaking with or coming to see one of your investigators, anything she might have said could be useful to our investigation. Ascertaining what might have been going on in her life that she may have kept hidden from her Bureau contact could prove pivotal."

"The name isn't familiar," Victoria told him, even as she turned the name over in her mind a second time, "but we'll double-check our records just to be sure. Under the circumstances, she may have used an alias to protect her identity."

"I'll e-mail a photo and a few other pertinent details for your use in discussing Ms. Brooks with your staff." Bailen stood. "Thank you, Victoria. I knew we could count on your agency for cooperation."

Victoria rose and offered her hand once more. "Of course, Detective. We're always pleased to assist Chicago PD any way we can. Please pass that sentiment along to your Bureau counterpart."

"Will do." Bailen gave her hand a final shake and made his exit.

Victoria felt certain Chicago PD and the Bureau would get to the bottom of this mystery, but the one thing she never did was leave anything to chance, especially if it involved her agency on any level. The Colby Agency would launch its own investigation.

And she knew just the man for the job, considering Witness Security had been involved.

Former U.S. Marshal Shane Allen.

Whoever Rebecca Brooks had been and whatever her reasons for becoming a homicide victim, the Colby Agency would find the truth.

Chapter Two

Shane Allen stared at the blinking light on the telephone for five seconds, which lapsed into ten, then twenty before he decided to pick up the receiver. He didn't want to take this call, now or ever, but he had little choice in the matter.

He pressed the blinking button and said, "Shane Allen."

"Mr. Allen, this is Harry Rosen, attorney for—"

"I know who you are," Shane interrupted. He didn't want to hear the man explain how he represented Shane's ex-wife. He also didn't want to hear how his petition for visitation rights was totally unfounded. It seemed impossible that the woman he had once loved could do this, but she had. Matt wasn't his son, but Shane had loved him for three years as if he were. It just wasn't fair that because the marriage had ended he was now supposed to stop loving the little boy and never see him again.

Nor was it fair that his former partner was the reason his life had gone to hell in such a hurry.

"Your attachment to Matthew is understandable," Rosen began. "But you have no legal recourse when it comes to Sharon's son. You surely know this."

Yeah, Shane knew. But that didn't mean he had to like it. He leaned back in his chair and forced himself to take a breath before he said something he would be sorry for later. "I suppose I was hoping Sharon would do the right thing since her son is the one who's going to be hurt by this battle." The kid's own father had already abandoned him without a backward glance. How was a five-year-old supposed to cope with losing the second person he'd trusted with his little heart?

The question infuriated Shane all the more.

"Mr. Allen, it would be in your best interest, as well as the boy's, if we moved past this issue. Sharon is relocating to Denver with her new husband, and there won't be any easy way for you to have access to Matt. Quite honestly, children of this age are rather resilient. Matt will forget all about you in a far shorter time than you realize…if you allow him to. I'm certain you have his best interests at heart. Do you really want him to feel unsettled any longer than necessary?"

Fury unfurled in Shane's gut. He wanted to reach through the phone and strangle this guy. Shane's relationship with Matt wasn't like last season's baseball statistics or an old toy to be set aside and forgotten. Didn't anyone see this besides him?

"I'll see you in court, Rosen," Shane warned. "Have a nice day." He hung up the phone and pushed to his feet. How the hell could the law allow this kind of thing to happen?

He paced the narrow expanse of floor space in front of his desk in an attempt to wear off some of the adrenaline. It didn't help. He stopped at the window and stared out at the November afternoon. Life went on even when things were damned wrong. Not that Shane still had any feelings for his ex—he didn't. Not in the least. But the kid...well that was a different story. He couldn't just pretend he didn't love the boy. Shane couldn't imagine never seeing Matt again.

A quick, short burst of sound echoed from the phone on his desk, alerting him to an internal call. Until the official hearing, there was nothing he could do. He might as well focus on work. He crossed to his desk and picked up the receiver. "Allen."

"Mr. Allen, this is Darla."

The new receptionist. She still addressed everyone at the Colby Agency as mister or missus. He'd done that, too, for the first couple of months.

"Have I missed an appointment?" He didn't remember anything on his calendar this afternoon. Still, he double-checked even as he asked the question.

"No, sir. There's a visitor in with Mrs. Colby-

Camp, and she would like you to join them in her office if you're available."

Sounded like he had a new assignment. Whenever he was called to Victoria's office, it usually involved an incoming case. He could definitely use the distraction. Working a case would keep his mind off Matt…and the hearing…and his ex.

"I'm on my way." He thanked Darla and settled the receiver back into its cradle. Taking a moment, he cleared his head of personal issues, then grabbed his notebook and headed for the boss's office.

The long stretch of corridor outside Shane's office went in both directions and was flanked by doors on both sides. At the end, near the stairwell, was Victoria's office. The layout was similar to the one in the old building, according to his colleagues. The décor was cutting-edge contemporary with a definite elegant flair. Very different from the monochromatic beige of his last workspace as a U.S. Marshal.

Shane had hired on with the Colby Agency right after New Year's. His former career had ended as abruptly as his marriage eventually had. A gunshot wound had shattered his hip, catapulting him into multiple surgeries and months of physical therapy. Despite his insistence that he could handle the physical requirements of his job, he'd been forced into retirement. Sharon had dumped him once he was out of the woods physically, and he'd spent several weeks feeling sorry for himself.

All that had changed come New Year's. He'd made one of those resolutions people never kept—only he had been determined to keep his. He was looking forward, not looking back. No wallowing in what might have been.

He gifted Mildred, Victoria's assistant, with a smile and entered the private domain of the woman who had turned the Colby Agency into one of the nation's most prestigious private investigation agencies. A woman who accepted him as he was, denim and leather included. That was another New Year's resolution he'd made: to be himself—not some spit-polished stuffed shirt like he'd pretended to be for six years. Nope. Just himself.

This was what he did now. This was his future. *This* was who he was.

"Shane," Victoria said as he strode across her office, "thank you for joining us."

As the boss made the formal introductions, he shifted his attention to the woman seated in front of Victoria's desk.

"This is Mary Jane Brooks." Victoria gestured to her guest. "Ms. Brooks, this is Shane Allen, the investigator I was telling you about."

Medium height, too thin. Mary Jane Brooks looked to be mid- to late-twenties with long red hair that spilled down her shoulders in sassy curls. Her pale, pale skin offered a stark contrast to her vibrant blue eyes.

"Mr. Allen." Mary Jane thrust out her hand as he approached the chair next to hers.

"Ms. Brooks." He closed his hand around hers, didn't miss her tremble as their palms made contact. That she drew her hand away quickly signaled that he, or men in general, made her nervous. He felt certain he wasn't what she had expected.

"Ms. Brooks has come to us regarding her sister's death," Victoria said as Shane took his seat. "Her sister's remains were among the ones found in the rubble after the explosion at our former building."

Now there was some interesting and unexpected news. From the corner of his eyes, Shane considered the woman next to him. He'd noticed the detective from Chicago PD in the lobby earlier today, but hadn't heard any news regarding the visit. If Ms. Brooks had been made aware of the news around the same time Victoria had been, she had certainly wasted no time in looking into the matter.

"Really?" He allowed the word to reflect his surprise. "Was she a client?" he asked Victoria.

"There's reason to believe she may have attempted to contact this agency," Victoria explained, "but we have no record indicating she ever followed through. I've spoken with the entire staff employed at the time, and no one remembers the name or the face." To Mary Jane Brooks she added, "Detective Bailen of Chicago PD's homicide division was here earlier today, and he provided photo ID for that purpose."

"Rebecca was going into Witness Security," Ms. Brooks put in, her tone stilted. "She was supposed to testify against her former boss, but she disappeared right before the trial was set to begin."

Interesting. Shane still had contacts in his former career. He would see what he could find out about the case. "Can you give us a few more details about your sister's employer?"

"She was the administrative assistant to the CEO of Horizon Software." Ms. Brooks cleared her throat. "She discovered he had been selling the same software his company designed for the Pentagon to one of the country's enemies. She reported him to the FBI in late October of last year. The day before Christmas Eve she disappeared. I never heard from her again."

Shane recalled hearing something about Horizon Software and suspected charges of treason. The whole ordeal had been kept hush-hush until the key witness had disappeared and the case eventually had to be dropped. By then, he had already been employed by the Colby Agency and had only gotten the scoop provided to the media.

"I don't know any specifics about the case," he said to Ms. Brooks before turning his attention to Victoria. "But I can try and reach out to some of my former colleagues. Depending on whether there is any hope of reopening the investigation, I may or may not be able to negotiate any useful information."

To Shane, Victoria showed her approval of his proposed strategy with a nod, while to the woman seated next to him she said, "Detective Bailen offered a possible connection between Rebecca and our agency. Evidently the cell phone of one of her close personal associates had been used to call our agency a couple of times. His name was Jason Mackey. Mackey was scheduled to perform at our annual Christmas party last year. But then he was one of three men who lost their lives to the perpetrators involved in the bombing of the building. Does his name sound familiar to you?"

"Jason Mackey was Rebecca's boyfriend," Ms. Brooks said without hesitation. "They'd been seeing each other for a couple of months when she went missing."

"So they became an item," Shane suggested, "after she turned Horizon Software in to the federal government for possible treason?"

Ms. Brooks shook her head. "Right before. I'd guess they had been dating maybe a couple of weeks when Rebecca decided to go forward with her plan."

Shane recognized the potential for a possible set up, but things weren't always what they seemed. It was possible that Mackey had nothing to do with what had happened to Rebecca, but that was definitely the first place, right after Rebecca herself and her former employer, that Shane would start looking if assigned to the case. That it appeared to Mary

Jane that the couple had started seeing each other prior to Rebecca's decision to thwart her boss might only be because Mary Jane hadn't known her sister's intent until well after the decision had been reached. "Was the relationship serious?"

"I think so," Ms. Brooks said hesitantly. "Rebecca was stressed about the trial. She didn't talk to me very much those last few weeks." She clasped her hands in her lap. "And I was a little busy, so I didn't push it."

If she planned to leave that statement hanging she should think again. "Busy in what way?"

Mary Jane Brooks looked from Shane to Victoria and back. "Our parents were ill. I was their full-time caregiver."

Was. "Who takes care of them now?" Shane needed specifics. Anything that related to Mary Jane's life might have impacted her sister's.

"They passed away."

The undeniable shine of emotions in her eyes made him wish he hadn't needed to ask the question.

"I'm very sorry for your loss," he offered. That was a real shame. The woman had lost both her parents and now her sister. Talk about a triple whammy.

"What kind of relationship did you and your sister maintain?" Victoria asked. "Specifically, those final months before her disappearance. You indicated that you didn't talk very often."

Shane was glad Victoria had asked the question. He didn't want to sound insensitive, and, coupled with the question he'd just asked, that one likely would have come across as unfeeling or accusatory.

"We were close on some levels," Ms. Brooks said. More of that hesitation. "Not so much on others."

"Can you elaborate?" Shane prompted. This was territory the lady clearly didn't want to go into, which told him in no uncertain terms that all was not as it should have been between the sisters.

"Rebecca loved our parents a great deal, but she didn't have the patience for taking care of their needs. Her financial resources allowed me to take an extended leave of absence from work and do what needed to be done. That arrangement put a bit of a strain on our relationship," she confessed. "But we got past it, and I believe we were as close as most sisters. Still—" she shrugged "—I recognized that there was an aspect of her life that Rebecca never allowed me into."

"Did you perceive that the things she kept from you were work related?"

Ms. Brooks considered Victoria's question for a moment. "That, and, during those final weeks, her social life. We'd always discussed boyfriends and such in the past but with Jason that changed."

More of those telltale signs of a possible setup: estrange the victim from those closest to her. "So, you didn't know Jason Mackey at all?" Shane suggested.

Mary Jane shook her head. "I only met him once. But I knew that Rebecca was a little afraid of him."

"Did your sister say she was afraid of him?" Shane pushed. "Or is that your perception of how she felt about him?"

"A couple weeks before she disappeared," Ms. Brooks replied slowly as if she were taking pains to answer accurately, "she told me that he had been tense. That he made her nervous when he got that way." Mary Jane turned to face Shane more fully. "You had to know my sister, Mr. Allen. She wasn't afraid of anyone. This was not like her at all. I asked her why she didn't break it off, and she refused to talk about it."

"Anything else you might think of would be very useful," Shane assured her. "Make notes whenever anything at all comes to mind. Frankly, my initial assessment would be that her former employer is responsible for her death, but your feelings regarding the boyfriend muddy the waters to some degree. I would suggest moving forward under the assumption that either one could be responsible."

"The truth is all I want," Ms. Brooks insisted. "She would do the same for me." She looked to Victoria. "After Detective Bailen gave me the news about the possible connection between my sister and your agency, I did a little research. The Colby Agency is the best. I want you to find out what happened to her. So, how do we do this? I'm sure there's a retainer fee."

"Under normal circumstances," Victoria agreed,

"there would be a retainer fee. But this case is different. I had already decided that we would launch our own investigation after Detective Bailen's visit today. There won't be any fees involved with our taking this case, Ms. Brooks. We need the truth, as well."

The lady's relief was undeniable. "I appreciate that, Mrs. Colby-Camp."

Shane's senses went on alert. Something in her voice had changed. The change in inflection was so subtle that he might have missed it had he not noted the shift in her posture. She sat up a little straighter, poised for battle.

"But," she continued, "you see, I need to be involved in this investigation. *Fully* involved. That may change the way you see things."

Shane and Victoria exchanged a look.

Since Victoria was the boss, Shane let her take the lead. She asked, "Involved in what way, Ms. Brooks?"

Shane watched her chin tilt slightly as she braced to argue her position.

"My sister was murdered," she said, "possibly for nothing more than her desire to do the right thing. As far as I can tell from the past eleven months, the only thing the authorities are worried about is finding a way to reopen their case. They don't care about my sister. And I doubt that Chicago's finest will get very far with the FBI and the U.S. Marshals running things to facilitate their own interests. I don't want Rebecca forgotten, and that's exactly what I believe will happen unless someone goes into this investigation with her interests as their primary goal."

"Solving your sister's murder would likely prove helpful to the Bureau's case," Shane countered. "Certainly, bringing down Horizon Software will be their goal, but don't believe for one second that Rebecca will be forgotten." He had to give credit where credit was due. Federal law enforcement took a bum rap for a lot of things. He couldn't in good conscience fail to speak up when he was all too well aware of protocol.

Mary Jane Brooks shifted her attention to him. The doubt was crystal-clear in her eyes. "That may be, Mr. Allen. But I need to be sure. I'm not taking any chances where my sister is concerned. I want the truth. The whole truth. Not some version that serves the best interests of anyone else involved."

"Rest assured, Ms. Brooks," Victoria cut in, "we will find the truth, and it will not be diluted by anyone's influence. You have my word on that."

Shane couldn't say whether or not Ms. Brooks understood what she was getting when she got Victoria Colby-Camp's word, but he hoped she understood exactly how significant the offer was.

"Then you won't mind if I follow this case with your investigator," Ms. Brooks countered, a hint of defensiveness in her tone. "Generally when there's nothing to hide, full disclosure isn't a problem."

"Full disclosure and shadowing an investigator," Victoria reminded her, "are two very different things. Ms. Brooks, there are safety issues that cannot be ignored. We have to assume whoever murdered your sister doesn't want to be revealed. Any attempt to do so will likely have dangerous repercussions."

"I'm aware of that," Mary Jane returned crisply.

"You need to consider carefully what you're asking," Shane said, jumping in and reiterating Victoria's words. If this was going to be his case, and it seemed it would be, he had no desire to be saddled with a civilian. Especially not one emotionally connected to the victim.

The would-be client didn't so much as spare him a glance. "I have to do this," she announced, undeterred. "If you can't allow me to participate, I'll be forced to go to another agency."

That could present a whole other set of problems. Not the least of which was the source of personal information the woman could provide.

"Ms. Brooks," Shane spoke up again, "we completely understand your concerns."

"You can't possibly." All signs of hesitancy or uncertainty were gone now. She looked at Shane with something bordering on contempt. "My sister was murdered. To the police this is just another case in a city where there's likely to be another murder later today. And another one tonight and maybe tomorrow."

Her hand rested against her chest, over her heart. "She was my sister. I need this done right. For *her*."

Shane looked to Victoria for confirmation before making a move he would likely regret. Victoria gave him a single, slight dip of her head as authorization to proceed as he saw fit.

"All right, Ms. Brooks," he relented with a heavy dose of lingering doubt as to the intelligence of the move. "You've made your wishes perfectly clear. I'll do what I can to facilitate your request. But—" he fixed her with a gaze that said his terms were non-negotiable "—you will be required to operate under my rules. No exceptions. What I say goes one hundred percent of the time. I make the decisions and set the pace."

Surprisingly, she thought about his offer for a time before responding. He had expected her to jump at the chance.

"As long as your rules don't prevent me from knowing and comprehending each step taken. I won't be left in the dark, Mr. Allen."

She'd definitely thrown down the gauntlet. The depth of her strength startled him just a little. She looked so delicate and fragile on the outside.

He might be about to make the first major mistake of his new career, but this woman had pretty much left him without any alternatives.

"Then we understand each other, Ms. Brooks," he confirmed. "We'll start today. If—" he directed his attention back to Victoria "—that's what you had in mind, Victoria."

She gave him another succinct nod of endorsement. "The sooner the better." Her gaze moved between them. "For all involved."

Mary Jane Brooks stood and turned to Shane. "I'd like to start with Jason Mackey. I'm certain he's the key to what happened."

Oh, yeah, he'd definitely made a mistake. Sixty seconds into the agreement, and she had already broken his first rule.

Chapter Three

Shane Allen did not look like any of the U.S. Marshals Mary Jane had seen on television or in real life. Not that she had seen that many, but she had been interviewed by two shortly after her sister's disappearance. Once the marshals had realized she didn't know anything, they hadn't visited or called again, nor had they returned her calls whenever she'd tried to get information about her sister's case.

Mr. Allen wore his hair long, almost to his shoulders. Dark and full, he made no effort to restrain the wavy length. A goatee on his chin drew her attention to the strong lines that delineated his square jaw. He looked not only dark…but dangerous. She resisted the urge to shiver.

He was not at all what she had expected.

Where was the tailored suit and polished oxfords? She'd noticed a couple of other Colby Agency employees while she had waited to see the woman in charge, and all had been dressed in a very businesslike manner. But not Mr. Allen. In contrast, he had worn jeans and a V-neck navy sweater over a white T-shirt. In lieu of oxfords he wore black leather boots, evidently to coordinate with the black leather jacket he'd donned as they had left the tenth floor.

In the parking garage of the Colby Agency building she had gotten another surprise: he drove a Harley.

A motorcycle!

Why would Victoria Colby-Camp assign this man to her sister's case? Was he as reliable, as *good* as the men she'd seen dressed in their classic suits? Or was she getting the low man on the totem pole because no money would be changing hands?

Mary Jane shook off the questions. She had to give this investigator the benefit of the doubt. Looks could be deceiving. She had learned that the hard way. Every single associate in her sister's life had worn the power suits and the polished smiles, and her sister was dead—murdered by someone from that world. Judging anyone by their outward appearance was clearly a mistake.

Insisting on starting with Rebecca, Allen had followed Mary Jane to her sister's apartment building. He'd parked his Harley directly behind her sedan at the curb outside the prestigious address. Rebecca had lived well, but then she'd worked hard for all she had attained. And she'd given freely.

Despite the fact that Mary Jane was the one

who'd had to set her career aside to take care of their parents, Rebecca had insisted on paying her full salary and any other involved expenses. How could she hold her sister's lack of patience with children and the elderly and ailing against her? Some people just weren't cut out to be caregivers.

Mary Jane's eyes welled with emotion as she strode up the walk to the front entrance. Mr. Allen kept pace with her, but didn't ask any questions or make any comments. He'd left the helmet and gloves with the motorcycle, but he still looked a bit like a road warrior with the leather jacket and well-worn jeans. She reminded herself again not to be judgmental. He could be the best investigator on staff at the agency. He was a former U.S. Marshal.

But was *former* the key word?

He opened the full-view glass door for her as they entered the lobby. At least his manners appeared to be impeccable and *classic*.

"Good morning, Ms. Brooks." The security guard smiled broadly as Mary Jane approached. During the past few months she'd been here often enough to get to know the guards on all shifts.

"Good morning, Wallace." She produced a smile that lacked the sincerity of the guard's jovial one. "This is Mr. Allen." She indicated the man who paused next to her. "He and I are going to check on Rebecca's apartment." She hadn't told anyone here that her sister was dead. The news was too fresh for her to pass along so casually. Calling when she'd made all the other necessary contacts would have worked, but she just hadn't been able to talk about it to the folks here yet. The security personnel treated her like family, spoke of her sister the same way.

"Yes, ma'am." He pushed the register toward the edge of the counter. "I'll need you both to sign in and I'll need to see ID for you, Mr. Allen."

Mary Jane didn't miss the speculative glance the guard sent in Allen's direction. She could understand his misgivings. Shane Allen looked a little *sketchy*. And it was Wallace's job to protect the tenants of his exclusive building, or their belongings in the event of their absence…or death. An ache settled deep into her bones. Everyone she'd loved was dead now. Gone.

Forcing her thoughts away from the grief, she signed the register as Allen withdrew his ID. He didn't speak as Wallace considered the driver's license and Colby Agency identification.

When the security formalities were out of the way, Mary Jane thanked the guard.

"Ms. Brooks's apartment is a popular place this afternoon," Wallace said as he passed Allen's ID back to him.

Mary Jane frowned, surprised. "There's been someone here today?" Detective Bailen? She supposed she should have expected that. Confirmation of her sister's murder changed everything. Re-ignited the investigation into her disappearance.

"Chicago PD was here earlier. Two of those marshals," Wallace explained, "are still up there now."

Next to her, Shane Allen seemed to tense...to become wary. "That's good, actually," Mary Jane offered in an effort to cover her confusion at her companion's reaction. "I hope it means they're putting forth some renewed effort."

"Yes, ma'am." Wallace drew his register back to his side of the desk. "Miss Rebecca sure isn't going to be happy about all this coming and going in her apartment." He amended quickly, "Except for you taking care of all those fish and her plants."

Mary Jane barely kept the tears in check as she nodded her agreement before making the necessary parting comments. She walked stiffly toward the bank of elevators, reminding herself to breathe...to block the sad thoughts. She had to focus, to keep every iota of her attention on finding out what had really happened to her sister. She pressed the call button and, thankfully, didn't have to wait. The elevator car opened welcomingly and she stepped inside, then selected floor twenty-one. Allen followed.

The doors closed, ensconcing her and the investigator who looked nothing like she'd expected in a small, silent space that made her thankful for the reprieve. Under any other circumstance she would have been nervous at the idea of being in a closed space with a man who looked more like a devilish pirate than a professional businessman. But then she reminded herself that he came with the Colby Agency's backing. The best of the best, the cream of the crop. Those were the phrases repeated over and over on Google when she'd done her meager research.

For a moment she considered asking why the presence of the marshals bothered Investigator Allen, but other thoughts intruded and all other synapses failed. Her sister was dead. She wouldn't be coming back. Her fish and plants would have to be moved to Mary Jane's house. For months, she had pretended that Rebecca would be coming back at some point. Now she knew for certain that wasn't going to happen…ever.

"You've been coming by to water her plants and feed her fish for all these months?"

The question dragged Mary Jane from her painful obsessing. She didn't look at him, although she felt his gaze on her. "Yes. Someone had to do it."

"Almost a year. That's a long time to take care of someone else's place."

A very long time. But then she was used to taking care of others. She'd been doing it her whole life in one capacity or the other if the truth be told.

"She was my sister. There wasn't anyone else." She shrugged. "Until today, there was a possibility that she would be back at some point."

She was alone. Mary Jane felt that weight crush down on her shoulders. There was no one else. No close family, hardly any friends. It was difficult to keep friends when you had bedridden patients to see after. Eventually the invitations to socialize had stopped coming. Maybe the worst part was that she hadn't even noticed.

On the twenty-first floor, the elevator glided to a stop and the doors opened. Mary Jane led the way to 2118. She knocked once before unlocking the door since Wallace had said that two marshals were in the apartment. She didn't want to get shot surprising a couple of gun-toting U.S. Marshals while they did whatever they were doing.

Investigating a murder—that was what they were doing.

Mary Jane took a breath. Maybe she'd watched too many movies. Or maybe she simply didn't trust anyone these days. Surely federal investigators wouldn't whip out their weapons in a secure building like this. It wasn't even the scene of the crime.

Marshal Dan Bolton stood in the middle of Rebecca's living room. He was the one who had conducted the initial interview with Mary Jane when her sister had gone missing. "Hello, Marshal." She produced what was no doubt a dim smile.

"Ms. Brooks." Marshal Bolton looked past her to the investigator, who closed the door with a firm thud.

Two things happened simultaneously. Bolton's expression turned grim, and his partner, Derrick Mitchell, appeared from the direction of the bedroom.

"Well, well," Marshal Mitchell announced as his

gaze settled on Shane Allen. "If it isn't a ghost from the past. How's it going, Allen?"

Mary Jane paused near the sofa to glance back at the man who'd entered the apartment after her. She supposed she should have considered that these guys might know each other, but she hadn't. Not even for a moment.

Allen stepped forward. The tension radiating from him confused Mary Jane all the more when, clearly, it should have warned her that there was about to be trouble.

"It's going," he said in answer to the other man's question. Then he gave his head a little shake. "I guess now we know," he went on, his tone deep with antagonism, "why this case hasn't been solved in a timely manner."

"That's a bit of a cocky attitude," Mitchell tossed back, "for a man who got himself shot and forced into retirement." He looked from Allen to Mary Jane and back. "I hope Ms. Brooks isn't pinning her hopes on you."

Marshal Bolton took a step right, blocking Allen's path to his partner. "We were on our way out." He nodded at Mary Jane. "We'll let you know if we learn anything new, Ms. Brooks." Bolton turned his attention to Mitchell. "Let's go. *Now.*"

Mitchell glared at Allen as he passed him, but he didn't say more. Bolton closed the door behind them and the tension in the room was reduced to a more tolerable level. What in the world had that been about?

"I take it you worked with Marshals Bolton and Mitchell," Mary Jane said when the silence went on for a second or two too long. She wanted to ask about Allen's getting shot and the glaring tension between him and Mitchell, but that was none of her business. The only thing that mattered to her was finding her sister's killer. Unless it somehow affected his job performance, this man's past was none of her concern.

Eyes so dark they were nearly black stared at her. "We knew each other. Let's just leave it at that, Ms. Brooks."

The words were spoken carefully, as if he'd meticulously chosen each one. The grave expression that tightened his face told far more than his words. There was an ugly history between those two.

"Will anything about your past relationship with Mitchell cause any difficulties conducting this investigation?" She needed to know that up front. Solving the ambiguity of Rebecca's murder was far too important to take chances with an investigator who had an ax to grind. She would go straight back to Victoria Colby-Camp with her reservations if necessary.

"No."

She might have had doubts for a second or two, but the sheer determination in those dark eyes proved immensely persuasive and seriously unnerving.

"Okay. So…" She glanced around the neat living room. "This is Rebecca's place. What would you like to see first?"

Allen didn't immediately respond to her question. He walked around the cozy living room with its all-white furnishings and sleek fireplace. Rebecca's taste had always run to the stark and clean, very contemporary. It still seemed strange to be here without her even after all the time that had passed. Mary Jane knew if she went into the bedroom and opened a dresser drawer she would still be able to smell her sister's unique scent.

God, she missed her.

Don't think about her…focus on the details. Hoping to accomplish that, before she realized what was happening Mary Jane got caught up in watching the investigator move around the room. He didn't touch anything, but the way he examined everything with his eyes was so intimate that she found herself fascinated by his movements.

The dining area to the right of the living space was as colorless as the living room, making all the sleek, black granite and stainless steel of the kitchen a real standout. Allen gave that space the same meticulous consideration as if he were memorizing her sister's choices in design as well as wines.

When he moved toward the short hall leading to the bedroom and bath, Mary Jane followed. He visually inspected the single picture hanging on the wall in that cramped hall. A black-and-white print of Rebecca and Mary Jane as young girls. It was the only family photo on display in the entire apartment.

Rebecca's bedroom was as spartanly furnished and was draped in the same cool whites as the living and dining rooms. The king-size bed was exactly as Rebecca had left it, the linens smoothed to perfection and the pillows arranged artfully into an inviting mound. Her sister had been obsessive about the details in everything.

Mary Jane closed her eyes for a moment to block the tide of emotion rising inside her yet again. She couldn't let the feelings of sorrow and regret overwhelm her. She had to keep her attention fixed on the investigation. Emotions would only get in the way.

When her lids fluttered open once more, Investigator Shane Allen was watching her.

"This apartment has been searched repeatedly."

She nodded, although she suspected that what he'd said hadn't been a question.

"You've checked every drawer," he went on, "every closet, any files and notes."

Again, she nodded.

"I need you to look again," he said, moving closer, or maybe she just thought he'd moved closer.

He felt closer. His dark, dangerous demeanor overpowered the room.

"I've already been through everything," she confirmed. "There's nothing else to look at. Besides—"

she shrugged "—what could I hope to find that the authorities didn't?" The forensics teams who had scoured her sister's apartment were trained to find evidence. She wasn't. She'd tried and found nothing. Looking again would be a wasted effort. He should recognize that as well as she did.

"This time," he definitely came closer, "I want you to look through the eyes of your sister, not Mary Jane Brooks. Forget the idea of how hurt or appalled you are about what happened. Look at her things the way you would have when that picture was taken." He gestured toward the hall where the single photograph hung. "See what she wants you to see."

He wasn't making sense. She and her sister hadn't shared that kind of relationship since they were kids—ten and twelve—the ages they were in that photograph.

She couldn't do this. The concept was ridiculous. "I don't understand. What's the point?"

"She was your sister. You were what, two, two-and-a-half years apart in age?"

That he stood so close…close enough for her to feel the intensity in his eyes…didn't help. "You're confusing me. What am I supposed to be looking for?"

"Your sister was scared. She knew she was in trouble. She'd stepped up to the plate and gone to the authorities about her boss. She couldn't share the intimate details with you. It was too dangerous and you were busy. But she knew deep down—" he pressed a hand to his chest "—that she could count on you if she needed you. You were sisters. She trusted you to take care of your parents. She knew you would be there for her no matter what happened. That's what kept her going."

Her heart was pounding. Mary Jane threw her hands up. He was guessing…or maybe it was wishful thinking. "I'm telling you we didn't have that kind of relationship as adults. We didn't even talk often anymore. When we did, it was generally about our parents."

"But you were her sister." He surveyed the room once more. "The only tie to family visible in this entire apartment is a picture of the two of you together. Not a colleague or your parents, not a significant other or fiancé. *You.* Only you and her."

He couldn't be right. Sure, Rebecca had called every week to check on the folks. But in spite of living less than a half hour away, she'd come to visit only every couple of weeks or so. She was too busy.

"The picture doesn't mean anything," Mary Jane argued. He was wrong.

"In my experience as a U.S. Marshal—" Allen stepped back, giving her space "—a witness, especially a smart one, doesn't go in to blow the whistle on her boss without some kind of backup. A plan or evidence, maybe both, but proof and/or protection of some sort. Something that backs up what they say, just in case."

Mary Jane assumed there was evidence. "Wouldn't she have turned over any evidence at the beginning?" Wasn't that the way it worked? Why hadn't anyone else asked her those questions if what he suggested was so logical?

"Possibly," he agreed. "She may have turned over significant evidence. But that doesn't mean she didn't leave some kind of insurance behind. Something to cover her just in case things went south."

Mary Jane let go a heavy breath. "Okay, tell me what you want me to do."

"Think." He glanced around the room again. "Where would she hide something just for you? Someplace no one else would think to look?"

Her chest tight, Mary Jane walked around the room. She tried to remember how they'd played together as kids. How Rebecca had always, always beaten her at Monopoly. She'd sworn she was going to be a real estate tycoon or a banker when she grew up. They'd played games that lasted entire weekends, dragging out the inevitable. Rebecca always won at Monopoly or anything else they played.

"We played games," Mary Jane said as much to herself as to the man anticipating some results she couldn't hope to produce. "Oh." Her heart skipped a beat as she vividly remembered one game they had played. "We told stories at night, in the dark." Her mind went back two decades. "Whoever told the scariest story won. That was the only game where I could hope to win." Mary Jane had been a natural-born storyteller. Give her a word or a seed of an idea and she could build a story around it. Not that storytelling was really a game, but they had kind of made it a game.

"In the dark?"

There he went, moving closer again.

Her gaze sought his. "Yes. In bed at night. We'd hide under the sheets with the flashlight."

Allen broke the eye contact and moved to the bed. Before she could fathom his intent he'd started tossing aside the mound of pillows.

Confused even more but not about to let him see it, she helped. When the bed was free of pillows, he drew back the silk comforter, then the sleek white top sheet.

Mary Jane's breath hitched. "What're you doing?"

He gestured to the turned-down bed. "Lay your head where she would have. Inhale the scent she left on the sheets. Make yourself remember. Would she have left you something—anything—to help stop the bad guys in the event she wasn't able to? Did she trust or believe in you that much? She left the care of your parents totally in your hands."

The idea was ridiculous. Rebecca had left the care of their parents in Mary Jane's hands because she was too busy. "This isn't—"

"Just try, Mary Jane," he urged. "I'll bet your sister had a lot more faith in you than you do."

That he called her by her first name rattled her. This was too confusing…too painful.

But she wanted the truth, didn't she?

She climbed onto the sheets and picked up her sister's pillow. With the cool satin pressed to her face, she inhaled deeply.

Yes, she could smell her. Mary Jane closed her eyes and let the memories bombard her. The bed was soft and welcoming, like the one they had shared as kids.

"Think," he urged softly. "Did she give you anything or tell you anything during those last weeks that might not have meant anything at the time but could now? It could have been related to your childhood."

Mary Jane started to say no, but a memory pinged her. The Monopoly card.

Park Place.

"Park Place." Mary Jane opened her eyes but kept the pillow hugged to her chest. "She sent me the Park Place card from a Monopoly game. It was tucked into a Thanksgiving card. I thought she was trying to cheer me up because the holidays were coming and our mother was so sick. There wasn't going to be the traditional dinner."

"Does that location mean anything to you?"

Her throat felt as dry as sand, but somehow she managed to speak. "It's one of the top properties on the Monopoly board. It takes a lot of money to buy it." Lines of concentration nagged at her brow. "There was a note in the card about it. Rebecca said something like, this will be yours one day…it's everything I have to offer." Why would her sister leave a message like that? At the time she had been too involved in her mother's swift deterioration to consider the card at length. She shrugged. "I thought maybe she was planning to try buying me a new house. She always said my place was too small." Another shrug. "Like I said, I thought it was some kind of overture to cheer me up."

"Besides Monopoly and the prospect of a larger home or financial security," Allen prodded, "does Park Place mean anything else to you?"

Mary Jane opened her mouth to say no, then she snapped it shut. *Park Place Towers.* Exclusive condominiums. A fellow teacher at her school had married a man who'd just purchased a home there. Mary Jane didn't remember mentioning that and she didn't recall hearing Rebecca comment on the new, exclusive property. The name could be coincidence. This whole exercise Allen had prodded her into could mean nothing. But she couldn't push the idea aside without ruling out the possibility.

"There's one place." She allowed her eyes to meet his. The impact unsettled her just a little. She'd never met a man quite so intense. The idea that they were focused on the bed and that she sat in the middle of it suddenly felt too intimate. She scooted off and put some distance between her and him. "Park Place Towers," she said in response to his question, "just off Lakeshore Boulevard. I don't remember discussing the place."

"We'll start there." As he made the statement he began to smooth the sheet back into place.

She started to ask why he would bother, but the probable reason crystalized before she could. To prevent anyone from knowing what they had done. Mary Jane helped him put the bed back to order just as her sister had left it. Nothing out of place meant no questions from the feds. Was that, she wondered, because of the tension between him and Mitchell?

"Does anything else come to mind? Any other place you might want to look?" he asked as they returned to the main living area.

"Should we check the back of the photo?" Rebecca could have hidden something in the frame behind the photo. Why was it she hadn't thought to consider that possibility before? Had she just assumed that the police would do their job and all would be set to rights?

Yes, she had. But that was before she'd been forced to face the reality that her sister was really dead.

Murdered.

"We can," Allen allowed, "but chances are, the forensics teams that have been through here checked there already."

She started to argue the point but he headed her off.

"Trust me," he said, "they wouldn't leave anything to chance. The property card your sister sent you may not mean anything at all. But, on the off chance it does, we'll check it out. If the place had particular meaning for you, and your sister knew that, then we may have a real lead. Right now, it's only a hunch. One no one knows about but the two of us."

His voice, deep and too intimate, got under her skin way too easily. She pushed the feeling aside. "Okay. So, now we go there?"

"We go there."

When they had locked the apartment, they made their way to the elevators. The silence during the ride down made Mary Jane uncomfortable this time. She thought of at least a dozen questions she wanted to ask but didn't.

In the lobby they signed out, and she endured Wallace's condolences. Evidently one of the marshals had told him that her sister was dead. Mary Jane promised to keep him apprised of the investigation and the memorial service.

She hadn't even had time to consider how she was going to handle the latter. It wasn't like the timing would be difficult. There wasn't any close family to invite. A few friends, but a scarce few.

Abruptly she realized what this meant on another level—when she died there wouldn't be anyone to take care of the arrangements or to attend the service. Her collection of friends was even smaller than her sister's and was dwindling fast. Sad. So sad.

How did one reach the age of twenty-nine and be so completely alone?

It was dark outside. Dark and cold. Mary Jane shivered as the wind cut through her coat. She wished she had remembered to wear a scarf.

"I'll follow you," Allen said as he moved toward his Harley.

"I'm not certain of the exact address," she admitted as she skirted the hood of her car. "But it's a popular high-rise, so it shouldn't be difficult to locate."

She'd clicked the unlock button and reached for the door before she noticed the flat tire. The aluminum wheel on the front driver's side practically sat on the ground.

"Oh, hell," she muttered.

"You got a spare?"

She jumped at the question asked over her shoulder.

Allen held out his hands in a calming motion. "Sorry, I didn't mean to spook you."

He'd moved up behind her as quickly and soundlessly as exactly that—a ghost.

"Yes." She took a breath. "I have a spare."

She couldn't remember the last time she'd had a flat tire, but she did know there was a spare in the trunk.

As he reached for her keys, his fingers brushed hers and she trembled again. The wind, she told herself. It was arctic-cold out, and she was unnerved after being in her sister's home and climbing into her bed. She'd been shivering and shuddering repeatedly.

She really needed to pull herself together a little better. Focus. Hold on to proper perspective.

He'd opened her trunk and removed the necessary implements before she had the presence of mind to ask if she could help.

"I've got it." He crouched down by the deflated tire and prepared to jack up the car. He inspected the flattened rubber for a moment first. "You have any enemies you know of?" He looked up at her.

Enemies? She shook her head. "No. Course not. Why would you ask that?"

He scrutinized the tire, then looked back at her once more. "Because someone slashed your tire."

Chapter Four

Park Place Towers was in the vicinity of Lakeshore Boulevard and appeared just as upscale as it sounded. A gleaming high-rise with an exclusive setting amid one of Chicago's wealthiest and most famous neighborhoods.

Shane followed as Mary Jane parked her car next to the curb in front of the building's main entrance. Again, he stationed his Harley behind her vehicle. While he removed his helmet and gloves, she climbed from behind the wheel of her car and studied the spare tire, made for emergencies, not aesthetics.

Her shock had been palpable when she'd realized that he was right, someone *had* slashed her tire. He doubted the conservative teacher had ever experienced such an affront against her person or property.

It was entirely possible that the vandalism had been random, but his instincts were buzzing with the opposite impression. Someone had sent the woman a warning.

He wondered if she had already been receiving warnings and simply hadn't recognized them as such. But then, she'd only just learned that her sister was in fact dead this morning. Unless she had been doing some major digging into her sister's where-abouts or someone suspected her sister had given her information, there would have been no reason for her to have been considered a risk.

But with her visit to the Colby Agency and being seen with Shane, she was now a definite risk to whomever didn't want the truth about her sister to come out. That person or persons would assume that she possessed some rationale for pursuing this route. And that could mean only one thing: someone had been watching her in anticipation of exactly this. The feds? Maybe. Until her sister's death had been confirmed, there was always the chance the woman was alive and might contact her only living relative. Those going into Witness Security sometimes got cold feet. Mary Jane had likely been under surveil-lance since Rebecca's disappearance for that reason.

As they reached the front entrance, she hesitated, let her gaze meet his. "Do you have a suggestion as to how I should approach this?" Her slender throat worked with the difficulty of swallowing. She was nervous. He could understand that. Murder was out of her comfort zone.

He considered her question a moment, then gave her the straightforward tactic he preferred. "Identify yourself and explain that you're here for Rebecca Brooks. They won't give you her number, but they'll offer to take a message or put through a call to her residence. If she doesn't own property here, you'll be told no one by that name is a tenant. Then we'll know."

She nodded. "Okay."

Shane reached for the door and held it open. She hesitated for only a moment before going inside, but that moment was long enough for him to see her hands shake as she grasped her purse more tightly.

The security desk clerk glanced up as they approached his station. "May I help you?"

Mary Jane moistened her lips. "I'm Mary Jane Brooks and I'm here for my sister, Rebecca."

She did great until the end. Her voice warbled when she said her sister's name.

The frown that claimed the security clerk's expression put Shane on alert.

"Ms. Brooks, may I see some ID?"

That meant only one thing, there was definitely a connection here.

Mary Jane placed her driver's license on the counter and waited while the man visually scrutinized the information and picture, assessing it against the woman waiting expectantly.

The clerk passed the license back to her and smiled. "Ms. Brooks, there's a message for you. It's been in holding for quite some time."

Mary Jane's heart started to pound. "A message?"

The gentleman behind the desk removed an envelope from someplace beneath the counter and passed it to her. "And this is your key and access card." He placed both on the counter. "Fourteen-ten. You may take either elevator to the fourteenth floor."

Her key and access card?

Mary Jane wanted to ask him what this meant, but right now she just needed to get to the condo he'd indicated and open this envelope.

She accepted the items. "Thank you."

She felt Investigator Allen behind her as she made her way to the elevator. Speech was impossible at the moment. If she said a single word she would break down. The security guard didn't need to witness that. He would have questions. Questions she couldn't answer.

When the elevator doors had closed, providing much-needed privacy, she prepared to rip open the envelope.

A broad, male hand closed over hers. "Not here."

Her eyes met his in question, and then she noticed the security camera. Of course. All public areas in a condominium high-rise this exclusive would be closely monitored.

She clutched the envelope and key to her chest and tried hard to relax. Her heart raced in spite of her best efforts, and her throat had gone furiously dry.

Why would her sister have purchased a luxury

condo in *her* name? Rebecca made good money and had an enviable savings…but she wasn't this well off. Was she?

How could Mary Jane not have known about this? What else about her sister did she *not* know?

The doors opened on the fourteenth floor, and Mary Jane took a deep breath before stepping out. The long corridor was lushly carpeted to muffle the sound of foot traffic. The walls were draped in something that resembled silk. The doors were wider than the average entry door and marked with brass numbers.

Mary Jane stopped in front of the one designated as 1410. She told herself to open the door. To go inside and to hope there would be something, a note, a recorded message—something—that would explain what this was about. But she felt paralyzed.

"Would you like me to go in first?"

She started at the sound of his voice. She'd been so lost in thought she'd completely forgotten he stood right behind her.

Before she could change her mind she thrust the key at him. "Yes. Please."

Taking a step back, she watched as he, using his right hand, inserted the key and gave it a turn. Then, with his left he twisted the knob. The door opened and he went inside. Mary Jane stood at the threshold for a few seconds, five or ten, she couldn't say for sure, before taking a step inside.

The front room was as grand as expected. A wall of glass overlooked the lake. Luxuriant carpet spilled across the floor of the empty space.

No, not completely empty. A small television with VCR sat on the counter of the built-in bookcases. As Investigator Allen moved through the rest of the condo, Mary Jane walked over to the television and turned it on. She couldn't say why she did that. Maybe to fill the emptiness with noise…maybe instinct had driven her to do so. A light indicated a video cassette was in the player. She pressed the play button and stepped back to watch, her movements stiff, jerky, her fingers ice-cold and trembling. Maybe all the condos had such a setup to welcome new tenants.

The TV screen blurred, and then Rebecca's image came into view. Mary Jane's heart seemed to stall in her chest. Her legs gave way, forcing her to drop to her knees in the lush carpet. Tears bloomed on her lashes.

"Mary Jane." The taped version of her sister smiled and appeared to gather her composure. "If you're watching this tape then you've realized what the Park Place property card meant. I pray it's you watching and not…" She cleared her throat and blinked repeatedly. "This place is for you. I know how hard you worked taking care of Mom and Dad and how much you gave up. So, this is my gift to you."

Mary Jane reached out and touched the face on the screen. God, how she missed her family. She was alone. So alone. Those blasted tears rolled down her cheeks.

"Give up the lease on your apartment and sell the family home," Rebecca's recorded voice ordered. "Put the money in the bank and go back to school and do what you always wanted to do, get your master's in social work. You deserve that opportunity." Another pause as her sister visibly conquered her emotions. "If you can't do it for you, then do it for me. Consider it my last request."

Mary Jane's breath caught. Her hands went to her throat. Rebecca had known that she likely wouldn't survive. Why hadn't she said something? Why hadn't she let Mary Jane help?

Because their parents had needed Mary Jane. During those final months they had required constant care. Their father with his heart condition and their mother with her cancer. The two had died within weeks of each other.

"Now," Rebecca's message went on, "there's one other issue."

Mary Jane swiped the dampness from her cheeks and braced for the next revelation.

"If you've found this condo and this tape," Rebecca began, "that means that you're looking into what happened to me." Her sister's face tightened and all signs of vulnerability vanished. *"Stop."*

Another sharp breath hissed into Mary Jane's lungs.

"Stop this minute. If I'm dead, there is nothing, *nothing*, you can do to bring me back. Now, I know how you love trying to help people. Being the caretaker is your natural inclination. But this is different, MJ. Very different. Trying to solve whatever has happened could get you killed. So just stop. Let it go. Nothing you could do will matter. What's done is done."

Investigator Allen crouched next to Mary Jane. She couldn't look at him, not with her face wet with tears. She was glad he kept silent, choosing to listen to what her sister had to say.

"Walk away from the past, Mary Jane," Rebecca ordered. "Get on with your life. You've been taking care of everyone else your entire adult life. It's your turn now. For goodness' sakes, find a man and have sex! No one should die a virgin, and if you don't do something that's exactly what's going to happen."

Humiliation heated Mary Jane's cheeks. If her sister weren't already dead, Mary Jane would definitely kill her! How could she say that? Giving her credit, Rebecca had likely expected her to be watching this alone.

The idea that this intense stranger was mere centimeters away sent the heat surging back in her cheeks.

"Have fun!" Rebecca commanded in that authoritative tone that had gotten her all the way to the top at Horizon Software. "Live every day like it's your last. Trust me, you'll be sorry if you don't."

Another pause as Rebecca struggled with her emotions. "Now, do as I say, little sister. I love you."

The screen blurred as the recording lapsed into blank tape. Allen reached out and turned off the television. He stood and offered his hand to assist Mary Jane to her feet.

Swiping at her cheeks with the back of one hand, she reached for his with the other.

"Is there anything else I should know about?" She sniffed, and gathered her composure. He'd started exploring the condo the moment they arrived.

"Empty. Nice views. Large master suite. Cutting-edge kitchen. You'll enjoy living here." His lips twitched with the hint of a smile. "Your sister left you a nice gift." He held up a set of keys. "And I've got a feeling these go to another gift that may be stashed in the garage."

Dear God. Rebecca should not have done this. She must have liquidated all her assets. All her savings.

Because she had known she was going to die.

Mary Jane closed her eyes. How could she enjoy any of this, knowing how she came by it?

"I don't think your sister would want you feeling guilty."

Another big gulp of air. "So I'm just supposed to move on and forget about her?" Her gaze locked on those dark, dark eyes. Mary Jane shivered for the dozenth time in this man's presence. From the roller-coaster emotion ride, she tried convincing herself once more. She shoved back the idea that her sister had announced her virginal status to anyone who might be listening. Except that she wasn't a virgin…just a near virgin with barely enough experience to distinguish the difference.

Allen looked around the extravagant living space. "That's up to you. But your sister was right about one thing." His gaze settled on hers once more. "Continuing to dig around in what happened to her could get you killed. You've already been warned."

The slashed tire. "That could have been some kid being stupid," she argued.

"In that neighborhood? Maybe, but I don't think so," he countered.

She crossed her arms over her chest. "You know what I mean. It might not have anything to do with me or my sister."

"I do understand what you mean," he offered in a gentle voice that seemed strangely out of character for a man who rode a Harley. "But you need to understand this is not like the crime dramas on television. The good guys don't always win. Your sister wanted to protect you. You could let her. My agency will conduct this investigation. We'll provide you with a full report when we're done. You have my word on that. There's no need for you to be involved in the leg work."

No need. Rebecca had been her sister. Of course there was a need for her involvement. To even think otherwise was absurd.

"I'm not changing my mind, Mr. Allen," she warned. "I'm going to see this through. We had a deal. Don't try wiggling out of it now."

Shane knew when he'd hit the wall. The lady was determined. He could waste time continuing his attempts to dissuade her or he could get on with this investigation.

"All right." He surveyed the view beyond the wall of glass. Lights flickered against the dark water. "Let's take another look around here just to be sure we didn't miss anything, and then we'll go back to your place."

"My place?"

The uncertainty in her voice brought his attention back to rest on her. "Is that a problem?"

She cleared her throat. "Ah…no. I suppose not."

"I'd like to spend some time going over what you know of your sister's movements those final weeks before her disappearance. Talking about it could jog your memory. The slightest detail might be the one that makes the difference."

"Well…okay."

With immediate plans out of the way, Shane took his time going over the condo. He checked every possible hiding place. Every carpet edge was secure, allowing nothing to be slipped beneath it. Each shelf and cabinet accessible and clear of obstruction. There was nothing else to find.

When he finished, Mary Jane still stood at the

wall of windows, staring out at the night. "This is crazy," she muttered as he moved up behind her. "Our lives weren't supposed to turn out this way."

No one's ever was. Murder wasn't something people factored into their future plans.

"Rebecca thought very highly of you," he commented quietly, not wanting to stir up her emotions but needing to reaffirm what he hoped Mary Jane recognized. A person didn't go to all this trouble for someone she didn't care deeply about.

"I know." Mary Jane's sigh was long and weary. "I can't help wondering if she knew just how much I loved and respected her." She turned to face Shane. "We didn't talk about it. Not since we were kids. Seems so wrong now."

"Most people don't," he offered, knowing the words would be of little consequence against the walls of emotions no doubt closing in on her just then.

"If we could only know in advance that we were seeing or talking to someone for the last time, we could…"

"What?" he challenged. "Say all the things we really feel? Tidy up any loose ends? Unfortunately, nothing about life is ever that simple." He knew from experience. Though he hadn't lost anyone he loved, at least not through death. There were other kinds of painful loss, though. Like having the woman you loved cheat on you with your partner. The idea that she had stayed with him through his surgeries out of pity still tied his gut in knots. As soon as he had been well enough to live on his own, she had gone to her lover—his former partner.

But Shane had put that behind him ages ago. There was nothing left to debate in his personal life except visitation rights with Matt. And he would probably lose that battle. Still, he had to try. He owed the child and himself that much.

"Yes." Mary Jane held her ground on the subject. "There were things I wanted to say to my sister. Things I should have said."

Shane hitched a thumb in the direction of the television. "I think it's pretty obvious she knew you loved her."

Mary Jane closed her eyes and her posture wilted a little. She was tired. Emotionally drained. The best thing he could do for her right now was to get her home. Maybe the questions could wait until tomorrow.

"We should get out of here." He crossed to the television. "I'm going to take this tape. I don't think much can be gained from an analysis." He pressed Eject, and the tape slid out of the slot. "But it may prove useful." He pocketed the cassette and gestured to the door. "If there's nothing else you want to take a look at here, we can be on our way."

As they left the building, Shane noticed a different security clerk had come on duty. He called a good-evening to them as they crossed the expansive lobby.

Shane was reasonably sure he couldn't ever get used to living like this. Close supervision. Exclusivity to the point of fear since the rich, real or make-believe, were ready targets. The address alone was motivation for thugs looking to make fast cash. With electronic gadgets a dime a dozen on the streets, lowlifes were no longer deterred by tight security. To the contrary—they saw the job as a challenge.

Just to make sure they didn't overlook anything, he and Mary Jane visited the garage and checked out the pricey SUV Rebecca had purchased and left as a part of her gift. No notes, no recordings this time. Just a nice set of wheels that still had the showroom smell.

Outside, Shane walked all the way around Mary Jane's sedan and found no more slashed tires or indications of foul play. Then he said, "I'll follow you home."

He pulled on his helmet and gloves and slung one leg over the seat of his ride. When she eased away from the curb, he fell in behind her.

The route she chose took them to the west side. Not really a bad neighborhood, just a little on the low rent side of the housing market. A far cry from the Lakeshore condo they'd visited.

She parked on the street. He had to drive past her selected parking spot to find something. She waited near her car for him to secure his bike and helmet.

As he approached, she pointed to her building and said, "Third floor."

The front entrance was not secured. Anyone could walk in. She paused long enough to remove a large wad of mail from her box. Judging by the bulk of it she hadn't checked it in a while. Seemed strange that a woman who gave off such "organized" vibes would allow her mail to pile up like that.

As if sensing his conclusion, she remarked, "I've been packing things up at my parents' place. I come home so late at night that I'm usually too exhausted to care about the mail."

Understandable. He let her set the pace as they climbed the three sets of stairs. The fatigue had long ago made its appearance in her posture.

While she dug for her keys at the door, he surveyed the frame around it for any signs of forced entry. Nothing suspicious caught his eye.

"I'll go first, if that's okay," he suggested. He wasn't taking any chances with her safety.

She shrugged. "Suit yourself."

He flipped on a light as he entered the apartment. Small, neat. Carpet that had seen better days, well-used sofa and chair. The bookshelves were running over with books, and he didn't see the first sign of a television. Cream-colored walls loaded with framed photos. The furnishings and decorating leaned toward earthy, which didn't surprise him. Brown sofa, couple of green throw pillows. Curtains were a paler green and puddled on the floor at each end of the one window that looked out over downtown in the distance. He imagined in the spring and summer that the heavy coat of leaves on the trees would block the view of city lights she enjoyed in the winter.

She dumped the mail on the counter that separated the living room from the tiny kitchen. "Would you like coffee or tea?"

"Coffee would be good." He could use the heat as well as the caffeine.

While she prepared the brew, he studied the many photos of her and her family. Lots and lots of snapshots of her and her sister as kids. Not so many as adults. He backed up to the last photo he'd scrutinized. Something about it seemed wrong. The picture was crooked. He took the frame off the wall and turned it over. Whoever had put it together had slapped it into place, leaving the assembly cockeyed.

He found another that way. Then another. His pulse kicked into overdrive. And yet another thrown-together frame and photo.

That was when he began to look for other signs of a rushed but methodical search. He got down on his hands and knees. The coffee table and sofa had been moved very recently. The indentations in the carpet from their former position were visible. Whoever had moved them had failed to put them back in the same spots. Shane shook his head. Sloppy, very sloppy.

"Excuse me."

He looked up at the woman who'd spoken and who was now standing over him with confusion and suspicion battling in her expression.

"What are you doing?" she asked, suspicion gaining the upper hand and tightening her weary expression.

He got to his feet. "When's the last time you moved your sofa or your coffee table?"

"I…I don't know. Months ago, I guess." She stared at the furniture in question. "Maybe never. I'm usually in a hurry so I vacuum around things."

He pointed to one of the hastily framed photos. "Did you hang all these yourself?"

"Yes." She peered at the photo he'd indicated. "But I didn't leave it like that. Did you do that?" The suspicion gave way to uncertainty.

He shouldered out of his jacket and dropped it on the sofa. "We're going to need to go through your apartment one room, one item at a time."

"I don't understand." She surveyed the many photos she had no doubt carefully and lovingly hung.

"I think someone has been in your apartment looking for whatever they believe your sister may have had in her possession at one time."

Mary Jane visibly prepared to debate his conclusion but something held her back. Instead, she went on the defensive. "She didn't give anything to me. I hardly saw her those last few weeks." Fear had nudged its way into her voice despite her best efforts to ward it off. "She wouldn't even talk to me about what she knew."

"You know that," he explained softly, "but they don't. If someone believes you have information pertinent to the case your sister was scheduled to testify in, you could be in imminent danger."

"That's insane." She set her hands on her hips and looked around at her small, modest home. Irritation had chased away some of the uncertainty and fear. "Even if your theory held any merit, why now? Why not look for whatever they thought my sister had months ago?"

"Maybe they found out today that she was dead just like you did. Just maybe she took some insurance with her and someone thought she was long gone with it. But now they know differently."

A frown furrowed her brow. "So, since she's dead, they think she passed it off to me?"

"They won't let it go until they're certain your sister hasn't left behind any means of getting to them. As your sister's only living relative, you're the most likely suspect. We just have to make sure we find it, assuming it exists, before they do. While," he added, "keeping you safe."

She threw her hands up and visibly struggled to keep her emotions steady. "I need that coffee now."

Shane imagined she would need something far stronger than coffee when she found out he wasn't about to leave her alone without protection.

He would be staying the night. On her sofa or outside her door. Whatever. But he wouldn't be getting out of earshot of Mary Jane Brooks...not until he understood exactly what they were dealing with.

He wasn't about to let her end up like her sister.

Chapter Five

"How many ways are we going to go over this?" Mary Jane was exhausted. She dropped her head against the sofa back. She had told all she knew over and over. To the FBI. To the marshals involved with her sister's case. To Detective Bailen. And now at least twice to Investigator Allen.

Stationed in the chair across the coffee table from her, he leaned forward, the intensity in his eyes a stark counterpoint to her fatigue. "Ms. Brooks, I know this is difficult, but it's also necessary. My goal is to reconstruct those final weeks of your sister's life. To attempt to comprehend what might have been going through her mind. What her motivations were for any actions she did or didn't take. Assuming she did, why did she call the Colby Agency? No one recalls speaking to her."

Mary Jane put up her hands to stop him. "How do we know she spoke with anyone? Maybe she hung up when the receptionist answered." Fear might have kept Rebecca from going through with whatever request she'd hoped to make. Another wave of weariness washed over Mary Jane. She was so tired. Completely drained. She needed sleep. For all they knew, Jason Mackey could have made the calls as part of his setup. If he had killed Rebecca, dumping her at the Colby Agency that night would have been the logical step if he'd intended to try and show a connection between her and the agency.

But then, he'd been murdered before he had ever made it into the building for the Christmas party.

"Perhaps we should call it a night." Allen rested his forearms on his knees and visibly withdrew the push she'd felt emanating from his eyes. "You're tired. We can continue this in the morning."

He was determined to stay the night in her apartment.

Mary Jane wasn't sure how she felt about that. Her tire had been slashed. Her apartment searched…it seemed. Was it possible her sister could have been looking for something? Surely Mary Jane would have noticed at some point during all these months if that were the case. Since she hadn't, that could only mean that the search had taken place recently.

Was it possible that someone suspected she possessed a piece of evidence against Horizon Software? Or other information that might prove pertinent? If so, did she risk facing that threat alone? *If* someone had been in her apartment, they could return.

Her attention settled on Investigator Shane Allen. Considering the possibilities, did she allow this man—this stranger—to sleep on her sofa?

Better safe than sorry.

Mary Jane stood, the effort draining her further. "I'll get you a blanket and a pillow."

Before she could step away from the sofa, he pushed to his feet with an ease of flow that seemed contrary to his tall frame. "I know this isn't exactly comfortable for you," he offered. "But it is the right thing to do. I've worked situations like this many times, and avoiding any unnecessary risks is definitely the route to go."

She had spent approximately twelve hours with this man. She didn't know him. Had absolutely no reason to trust him beyond the fact that he was employed by a prestigious private investigation firm and yet…she did. Trust him, that is. On some level, anyway.

"I'm glad you're going to stay," she admitted. The words sounded a little shaky, but she meant them. Yes, putting the idea into action was a bit awkward. She hadn't had a man spend the night in her apartment since…

Actually, she'd never had a man spend the night in her apartment. She hadn't dated in ages. Who had the time or inclination when disease and death were your constant companions?

Mary Jane took a breath. "I'll be right back."

She made her way to the hall closet. The pillow and blanket she used sometimes when she crashed on the sofa were right where she'd left them the last time. Resting her hand on the pillow she considered that it had been almost two years since she had lived full-time in her apartment. She'd moved into her parents' home after her mother's cancer had reached a debilitating stage. Mary Jane was certain her father's heart had managed to keep working sufficiently for him to see his wife through her painful final months. Then, as if he'd completed his work on this earth, he'd died in his sleep less than one month after her burial.

That had been six weeks ago. Since laying her father to rest, Mary Jane had divided her time between settling things at her parents' home and taking care of the necessities around here. She'd ended up spending more time away than at home. Pressing her forehead against the door, she could confess now that she'd stayed at her parents' home maybe a little longer than necessary to be near the memories.

She was all alone now.

Completely alone.

Hugging the pillow to her chest, she reached for the blanket. As soon as Rebecca's murder was solved, Mary Jane had to get on with her life. She couldn't keep living in the past. It wasn't healthy.

It wasn't right. Neither her parents nor her sister would want her to live like this…in limbo.

But first, whoever had killed her sister had to pay. She was certainly no vigilante, but she wanted justice. Justice wouldn't bring Rebecca back, but it would make Mary Jane feel like she'd done the right thing by her sister. That was something she had to do…no matter the risks.

Back in the living room, Shane Allen waited right where she had left him. Standing. Watching. His stillness made her pulse react just a little. She wasn't afraid of him. Not really. She was just nervous, she told herself. Maybe as much about his suggestion that she could be in danger as by the idea of having a stranger in her home while she slept.

"Thank you." He accepted the linens.

"Good night." Somehow she managed a half-hearted smile. When she would have turned back to the hall, she hesitated as a question she'd wanted to ask earlier bobbed to the surface of her exhaustion. "Do you think—" she searched his face for an answer before she even completed the question "—my sister was afraid of more than the bad guys at Horizon Software?"

He considered her question for a time. She suddenly felt stupid for asking, but she had a right to know what conclusions he had reached thus far. He'd put in a call to one of his former colleagues, but the response hadn't been what he'd wanted. The open status of the case prevented his friend from discussing the details.

"If you're asking me if she might have felt she had been sold out by her protectors, that's always possible." He shrugged. "Anything is possible."

She hadn't noticed until then just how wide his shoulders were. Maybe the leather jacket had kept her from focusing on the actual breadth of him. Her entire life she'd always associated motorcycles—and those who wore battered leather and shabby denim—with rogues. But this man was a former U.S. Marshal. A member of the prestigious Colby Agency staff. A good guy. Maybe he'd become a bit of a rebel after leaving the Marshals Service. If she got the nerve, she'd ask. Eventually.

"Even the best man has his weakness," he went on. "If he permits it, that weakness can cost him everything."

The idea that he spoke from experience overwhelmed her ability to think rationally. "Has that ever happened to you, Investigator Allen?"

"Only once. But it won't happen again."

She didn't know where the question came from, but it was across her lips before she could stop it. "Is that why you're not a marshal anymore?"

For five, then six beats of her heart he didn't answer, just searched her eyes as if he could see—when she couldn't—the motivation behind her question.

"Yes."

"It wasn't drinking." Not a question. She somehow sensed that he was not the type to give in to drugs of any sort.

"No."

The flash of old pain in his eyes gave her the answer.

"A woman," she guessed.

"My ex-wife." He said this with such indifference that it was difficult to believe he would have been distracted by someone he clearly cared so little for.

Mary Jane wasn't sure how to respond. She'd un-questionably delved into sensitive territory for this dark, brooding man…who was set to spend the night on her sofa.

"I found out she was cheating on me," he con-tinued with the same matter-of-fact tone. "I was distracted and ended up in the path of a bullet. That's why I'm no longer a marshal."

"That must have been hard to deal with all at once." Losing the woman he loved and his career *and* recovering from an injury.

"Like I said, it won't happen again."

There were other things that she suddenly wanted to ask, but his closed expression was loud and clear: he had no desire to discuss the subject further.

"All right." She backed up a step. "Good night, then."

Mary Jane made it all the way to her bedroom

without looking back, although she wanted to. Her curiosity was definitely aroused now. She wanted to know what made this man so different from the others she had seen at the Colby Agency. So totally opposite to the marshals who had interviewed her in the past few months.

Had he veered close to death from the gunshot wound? Had losing his woman and his career sent him on a search for who he really was?

She closed the bedroom door behind her and sagged against it. Somewhere in the back of her mind she'd been toying with the idea that she needed to take some time to find herself. It seemed foolish. She'd gone to school to be an elementary school teacher. She had taught for five years before her parents had become ill, and she'd taken an extended leave. She had planned to return to teaching the next school year, some nine months from now. About the only work she could hope to get midway through the school year was substitute teaching. But the concept of doing a little soul searching and looking into other options still hovered in the back of her mind.

Maybe she would do just that.

Explore the possibilities and see if she was the same person she'd thought she was when she'd dived into an education degree. The insurance money would tide her over for some time to come. Rebecca had always said she deserved a break. Maybe she would travel. A long, relaxing cruise would be nice.

Mary Jane stripped off her blouse and slid down the zipper of her skirt. She pushed it to the floor and went in search of a suitable nightgown. In the event the building caught fire in the middle of the night, she didn't want to be dressed too scantily with a man sleeping on her sofa.

She tugged on a pink, ankle-length flannel one that looked exactly like something her grandmother would have worn. Then she brushed her teeth and washed her face before turning out the light and climbing into bed. She sighed at the marvelous feel of comfort and familiarity. It was good to be home.

The apartment was quiet, so she assumed that her bodyguard had gotten comfortable on her sofa. Her mind focused on her sister and the troubles she'd faced upon discovering those ugly secrets about Horizon Software. Rebecca had already made up her mind and gone to the authorities before telling Mary Jane anything. Even then, she'd only explained that there would be a trial and that Mary Jane was to speak to no one regarding her sister or her sister's work.

No one had questioned Mary Jane. If she'd been watched or followed she had not been aware of it. Then, just before Christmas last year her sister had disappeared. Vanished off the face of the earth as if she had never existed. It grieved Mary Jane to allow thoughts to surface of how she had died. She could only imagine the fear her sister had felt. No one should ever have to feel that way. What kind of animal enjoyed hurting another human being?

The shrill sound of the doorbell sent Mary Jane's heart rocketing into her throat. She bolted upright. Fear tightened in her chest. She had flung back the covers and crossed the room before her brain could catch up with her body.

Wait.

Investigator Allen would check to see who was at her door. She glanced at the clock on the bedside table. Eleven-fifteen. Who would show up at this hour?

Detective Bailen?

Was there more news?

Unable to bear the not knowing, she yanked open the door and burst into the hall.

A tall, male body stopped her. "Stay in your room until I find out what this is about."

The light from the living room reached far enough into the hall for her to get a good look at his expression. Grim. Determined.

"Is it a man or a woman?"

"A woman."

Someone she worked with? A neighbor?

She started to ask more when he grasped her by the shoulders and ushered her back into her room. "I'll let you know if it's safe to come out."

He'd closed the door before she could summon a response.

She couldn't stand here like this. She grabbed the clothes she'd shed only minutes earlier and quickly donned them once more. Whatever this visitor wanted, she needed to know. It could involve her sister.

Once she'd pulled her clothes into place and had taken a breath to calm her nerves, she cracked open the door and listened. The voices were too low for her to make out what was being said.

Slowly, one inch at a time, she opened the door and eased out into the hall. She stole her way as close to the doorway leading to the living room as she dared and then she held very still to listen.

"That's not possible."

Shane Allen's voice. Whatever the visitor wanted, he wasn't going for it.

"I have to speak to Ms. Brooks," the woman insisted. "I won't talk to anyone else."

"If you have information for Ms. Brooks, you'll have to pass it along through me." He held his ground, his tone unyielding.

"Look." The exasperation in the woman's voice multiplied. "The information I have to give her could cost me my job. Could get me sent to jail," she fairly shouted. "I'm not giving it to anyone but Mary Jane Brooks."

"Then we have nothing else to discuss," Allen concluded.

It was all Mary Jane could do to hold herself back. What if this woman knew something relevant to

Rebecca's murder? All she had to do was step away from the wall and walk into the living room. Three, four steps max and she could look this woman in the eye and demand to hear what she had to say.

Something like fear kept her plastered to the wall. She told herself to move, but she couldn't.

"This is ridiculous!" the woman argued. "What I have to say is extremely important."

"You're aware that Rebecca Brooks was murdered?" Allen countered.

"I heard it on the six o'clock news," the woman threw back at him as if she recognized that he was accusing her of having something to do with Rebecca's death.

"Then you're aware that there's a homicide investigation underway and that any knowledge you have about the victim could be relevant to that case. You could be obstructing justice by holding back."

Silence.

Mary Jane held her breath.

He was going to spook her. She wouldn't talk if he kept scaring her to death.

"I know the law," she snapped. "I know what I have to do. I just didn't want to go to the police before telling the sister. You know how the cops are, they'll tell her what they want her to know. I'll tell her the truth."

Okay. Enough.

Mary Jane stepped forward and walked

directly into the living room. "What is it you have to tell me?"

"Ms. Brooks, go back to your room." Allen stepped between Mary Jane and the other woman. "I've got this under control."

"Let her talk." Mary Jane stared straight into those dark eyes and showed him with her own that she was not taking no for an answer. She wanted to hear whatever this woman had to say.

He held her gaze for an extra beat, just long enough for her to doubt that he would allow her to have her way. Then he stepped aside.

Mary Jane searched the woman's face. Thin and pale, she looked to be in her late twenties, like Mary Jane, only there were deeper lines around her eyes and mouth as if she'd lived those years far harder. Dark roots betrayed her blond hair, and gray eyes reflected the weight of whatever was on her mind.

"My name is Cassie Scott. I'm a dental hygienist. I work at the Caldwell Dental Clinic downtown." She took a moment, wrung her hands together as if the next part had to be drudged up from deep inside her. "Last year I worked at the walk-in clinic over in Yates on the south side."

Mary Jane knew the area. Rough neighborhood. Ms. Scott had definitely made a move up this year. But what did any of this have to do with Rebecca?

"You said you had information for me," Mary Jane prodded.

Ms. Scott nodded. "I had a drug problem." She took a ragged breath. "Meth. It took months of rehab but I'm clean now."

It still startled Mary Jane when she heard about health professionals getting involved with such a nasty drug. They, of all people, should know better.

"Anyway—" Cassie shrugged "—this time last year my life was in a downward spiral, and I would have done just about anything to support my habit."

Mary Jane's senses stirred. "Something you did involved my sister?" Knots formed in her belly and she found herself unable to breathe.

Cassie Scott nodded. "A man approached me through my *source*."

Mary Jane's brow furrowed. "Your source?"

Cassie wet her lips. "My drug supplier."

Okay. She got that. "What did this man want?" Mary Jane wasn't sure she wanted to know where this was going…but she *needed* to know. Maybe Shane Allen had been right. Maybe he should have heard this first. No. She had to be strong.

"He wanted me to alter a set of dental records."

Mary Jane's heart started to thunder. "Whose dental records?"

"A patient at the walk-in clinic. He said she wouldn't need them anymore." The woman's hands shook even as she wrung them tightly.

"You presumed this woman to be dead?"

Mary Jane's attention swung to the man standing

beside her. He'd uttered the question she hadn't been able to string together quite yet.

Cassie nodded an affirmative. "I was afraid to ask."

"What did he want you to do with the dead woman's dental records?" Shane followed up.

Mary Jane had gone cold. Her knees felt weak, and she was sure she couldn't properly buttress herself for whatever came next.

"He wanted the views of the patient's latest X-rays, but first…he wanted me to alter the name on the views."

"So you altered the X-rays as requested, and he paid you for your service?" This time Allen's question held an obvious note of disdain.

"Yes." Cassie's expression turned pleading as if she needed him to understand. "I was desperate. I'd done a few small jobs for friends of my source before. Things I'd watched done enough times that I was pretty sure I could do it. Like an extraction or reseating a crown or bridge. But nothing—" she swallowed with effort "—like this. This could cost me everything."

"Who was this man who came to you?" Mary Jane asked—demanded, actually. She had to know if it was someone from Horizon Software. Maybe she wouldn't recognize the name, but surely Detective Bailen would. "And what does this have to do with my sister?"

"I'd never met him before," Cassie explained.

"He didn't seem like the usual type who asked for this sort of thing. He seemed…nice."

"His name," Allen pressed.

"Jason Mackey. I heard about his murder a couple weeks after that. It scared me to death, so I kept my mouth shut. He was dead. It didn't seem like it was relevant to the job I'd done for him…*until* today."

Mary Jane's arms went around her middle in an effort to hold herself steady.

"I heard about your sister," she said to Mary Jane. "That she was dead, I mean. It was all over the news tonight."

Emotion swam in Mary Jane's eyes. She still didn't understand what any of this had to do with her or her sister other than the fact that Jason Mackey was a scumbag and Mary Jane had already figured out that part.

"I'm clean now," Cassie reiterated. "I got my life back together, and I'm trying to do the right thing." She looked away. "I knew I had to do this."

Fear froze Mary Jane's blood. She wanted to ask what this meant. How it tied into her sister's murder. But her lips wouldn't form the words pounding in her brain.

"What was the name Mackey wanted you to put on the dental records?" Allen prodded before Mary Jane could summon any sort of response. His stern voice tugged Mary Jane from the pull of grief.

"Rebecca Brooks."

It took a few seconds for that reality to sink deeply enough to make any kind of sense and then anticipation seared through Mary Jane. "What are you saying?"

Cassie Scott looked from Mary Jane to the man beside her and back. "I'm saying that if the medical examiner used the X-ray views I altered to confirm your sister's identity, then they've made a mistake." She exhaled a mighty breath. "Those X-rays belonged to Amanda Ferguson, a prostitute I once did an extraction for to pay off my…my debt to my source."

Mary Jane's gaze locked with Shane Allen's. "What does this mean?"

He glanced at the other woman, then settled those disturbingly dark eyes back on Mary Jane. "It means the remains identified might not be your sister's."

Chapter Six

By midnight, Victoria Colby-Camp had assembled her two right-hand staff members, Ian Michaels and Simon Ruhl. Both men had been briefed on the recent developments. Shane paused as the woman next to him hesitated before entering the conference room. The past hour had been extremely difficult for Mary Jane Brooks. She had just learned that there was a possibility that her sister was not dead. As much as she wanted to believe this was good news, there was no evidence to support that conclusion as of yet.

The one thing they knew with any certainty was that nothing about this case was what it appeared. There were far too many unknown variables.

And if her sister wasn't dead, where was she? Why hadn't she contacted her only living relative?

The dental hygienist, Cassie Scott, had asked not to be identified unless absolutely necessary. Shane wasn't sure he could keep her name out of the investigation, but he would give it his best shot. The woman had turned her life around—going to prison wasn't exactly high on her priority list. Nor would it accomplish anything good.

As Shane introduced Mary Jane to Ian and Simon, Detective Bailen arrived.

"What's going on, Victoria?"

Bailen looked a little harried. Not surprising, since it was the middle of the night.

"Let's convene at the conference table," Victoria suggested as she indicated the polished mahogany expanse across the room, "and Mr. Allen will brief you on tonight's startling turn of events."

Bailen didn't look too happy about waiting the minute it took for everyone to be seated, but he kept any protests to himself out of respect for the woman in charge. Shane had noticed in his relatively short tenure at the Colby Agency that few dared to cross Victoria Colby-Camp.

Shane waited for Victoria's signal that he should begin, then he got straight to the point. "Earlier this evening I received an anonymous tip that the dental records used to identify the remains of Rebecca Brooks were unreliable."

Bailen's expression was openly suspect. "Clarify what you mean by *unreliable*."

"According to my source, the records utilized belonged to a woman named Amanda Ferguson and not to Rebecca Brooks."

The detective looked from Shane to Victoria and then to Mary Jane. "The records were provided by the dentist you said your sister had used for years," he reminded Mary Jane. To Shane he suggested, "This question of reliability may lie in your source."

"We acknowledge that this is purely hearsay until you can confirm the facts," Shane stated for the record and in an effort to keep Bailen focused on him. He preferred to have the detective's intense scrutiny away from Mary Jane. "But we felt this information could not be dismissed without due consideration. As you know, the law requires that we share this sort of discovery with the authorities. Starting with you seemed the right thing to do."

To Shane's surprise, Bailen nodded. "I agree." He settled his full attention on Victoria once more. "But I'm afraid I'm going to need to know more about the source of your tip if I'm to treat this information as sufficient motive to divert resources from the thrust of our current investigation. It's not Chicago PD's policy to utilize resources unless there is proper justification."

Mary Jane's posture stiffened noticeably. Hoping to reassure her, Shane placed his hand on her arm beneath the table. The jolt of something like electricity when his palm connected with her skin sent a startling rush of tension through him. The tiny hitch in her breathing told him she'd felt it, as well.

Shaking off the strange reaction, he zeroed in on

Bailen and called the man's bluff. "As a former civil servant, I understand exactly what you mean, Detective. Particularly at this time of year budgets are stretched thin. We'll look into the accusation and keep you posted. If the tip turns out to be of any consequence, we'll turn our findings over to you and your department for further examination."

"Absolutely," Victoria seconded. "I apologize for calling you in unnecessarily, Detective Bailen."

Surprise and then irritation played across the man's face. "Victoria, if you know more than you're telling me, we could have a serious problem here." His gaze swung back to Mary Jane, no doubt considering her the weakest section in the wall he'd just hit. "It would be in everyone's best interest to put all cards on the table here and now. What is it you're not telling me?"

The tension in the room thickened, but Shane knew they had the detective right where they wanted him. "I'm afraid that's all we have, Detective. I received the tip and this is it. Whether you check it out or not is up to you."

The standoff lasted ten seconds, then ten more. Shane didn't break eye contact. Bailen might have a couple of decades on him in the business of interrogation, but there was no way he could win. Shane was very, very good at this game. He had only lost his focus once, and that had been because he'd let his heart get in the way.

That wouldn't happen again in this lifetime.

Bailen pushed back his chair and stood. "Amanda Ferguson," he repeated. "I'll look into it." He glanced at Mary Jane. "The best place to begin would be with any other dental offices Rebecca may have used."

Mary Jane considered her words before she spoke. "I've given that a good deal of thought," she said, her voice shaky. "As I told Mrs. Colby-Camp, we lived in St. Louis before moving to Chicago sixteen years ago. I can't remember the clinic or the dentist, but I do remember that Rebecca wore braces in St. Louis." She clutched the edge of the table as if she feared she might not be able to remain steady without that anchor. "I definitely remember the braces."

Bailen exhaled a weary breath. "I'm sorry, Ms. Brooks, do you have any idea how many orthodontists there likely are in a city the size of St. Louis?"

Victoria pushed to her feet, drawing the detective's attention back to her. "Just over seven hundred dentists, with approximately seventy listed specifically as orthodontists. Our research department is already looking into the possibilities."

This time the standoff lasted less than five seconds.

"I presume you'll share your results with us," Bailen said, his resignation tangible.

"I'll have Mildred send an e-mail update directly to you every hour on the hour."

The detective shrugged. "All right. I'll let you

know if I find anything to back up your *anonymous* tip." He shot Shane a look that said he was well aware he hadn't gotten the whole story.

Shane didn't flinch. Prosecuting his source for mistakes she had made a year ago under the influence of drugs wouldn't serve any useful purpose now. As long as he could protect her, he would.

Victoria saw Bailen to the lobby and the tension in the conference room diminished considerably.

"I'll see how research is coming along," Simon Ruhl offered. "See if we have anything new." He checked his wristwatch. "I doubt we'll have much before noon. Most of the dental clinics won't open until nine, and many of the records more than a decade old will be in storage at this point."

Ian Michaels, a former U.S. Marshal himself, gathered his notes. "A twenty-four-hour turnaround is the best we can hope for." To Mary Jane he said, "I know waiting isn't easy, Ms. Brooks, but this kind of investigation requires patience and perseverance."

Mary Jane wilted a little as he said what no one in her position wanted to hear. As long as twenty-four hours seemed, it was a hell of a quick turnaround in a situation like this.

Ian shifted his interest to Shane, but before he could say what was on his mind, Ben Haygood rushed into the conference room.

"I got another usable hit on Amanda Ferguson."

Mary Jane watched as Shane Allen and his colleagues considered the latest information discovered on the prostitute whose dental records had allegedly been switched with Rebecca's. Mary Jane closed her eyes. This was all so unbelievable.

If her sister was alive, why hadn't she attempted to contact Mary Jane? Why hadn't she sent some message when their mom, then their father, had passed away?

Could Rebecca have deserted them so completely? Could she really have been that heartless and Mary Jane just hadn't noticed?

It seemed so impossible. Every instinct argued against that conclusion. Rebecca had been focused and ambitious, driven even, but she hadn't been uncaring or disinterested. Didn't that expensive Park Place condo prove that? If she were out there somewhere still alive, uncaring as to what happened to her family, wouldn't she have wanted all her money for herself?

Surely a woman capable of abandoning her entire family in their time of greatest need wouldn't be so selfless and generous. The condo. The vehicle. It didn't add up.

Mary Jane pushed those thoughts away and joined the others on the opposite side of the conference table. Whatever new information they had found, she needed to understand how it impacted Cassie Scott's assertion regarding the dental records.

"Extra-long rap sheet," Simon Ruhl commented

with a hint of regret in his voice. "Barely twenty-five, and this one was into some nasty stuff."

Ian Michaels indicated one entry in particular on the report. "Looks like there are several entries related to assaults where she bit clients."

Ben Haygood passed another document to Shane Allen. "The rap sheet's interesting," Haygood offered, "but this is the really incredible part."

Ian Michaels's brow furrowed as his expression darkened. "Is this what I think it is?"

Mary Jane could only see that the page contained a long list of what appeared to be names. Her pulse fluttered at the idea that they might be getting somewhere already. Whatever they could learn about Amanda Ferguson might give them some insight into what had really happened to Rebecca.

"It sure is." Shane Allen looked from one man to the next before visually connecting with Mary Jane. "This is a for-sale list."

Confusion further scrambled her already weary thoughts. "What's a for-sale list?"

His dark eyes fixed on hers. "It's a list of people who, for whatever reason—terminal illness or just plain desperation—are prepared to literally sell their souls to the highest bidder. Maybe they have family they need to help or some debt they want to settle. And they're willing to provide organs, alibis, anything to do it."

Disbelief sat like a lump of ice in her stomach.

"Amanda Ferguson let someone pay her to be murdered?" Dear God, what had Rebecca done?

Simon Ruhl flared his hands in a *maybe* gesture. "She's on the list, which means she was willing. Whether or not she did, we don't know yet."

"That list," Ben said as he tapped the one Ian held, "was posted last year. I found it on a Web site that was debating the legalities." He produced yet another sheet of paper filled with names. "This one is from the same source, only more recent." He pointed to the names. "No Amanda Ferguson on this list."

The chilling lump in Mary Jane's stomach expanded. "So, she's dead." Oh, God. That meant the remains found could be Amanda Ferguson's. Good heavens, how could Rebecca be capable of something like this? How could Mary Jane not have known just how desperate her own sister was?

She didn't realize she was backing away from the group until Shane Allen's strong fingers wrapped around her arm.

"Are you all right?"

"I need to go home." She couldn't be here right now. She needed to be alone. To think and sort this all out…somehow.

The shock of all she'd learned in the past two hours hit like a hard right jab square between the eyes. She swayed with the emotional impact.

"I should get Ms. Brooks home," Allen said to the others. "Call me if there's an update."

Mary Jane was vaguely aware that the other men made sympathetic overtures to her, but she couldn't find her voice to respond. Allen ushered her into the corridor and toward the lobby. The walls seemed to close in on her even as they walked quickly toward the large reception area. Her throat thickened, making a decent breath nearly impossible.

Rebecca could be alive.

She may have paid someone to die in her place. To protect herself?

Or was she somehow a part of the dirty business Horizon Software had been into? That didn't make sense. If she was a part of it, why go to the authorities and blow the whistle?

This was all crazy.

Not real life.

Not Mary Jane's life.

She was a school teacher from a quiet, Christian family who never even swore, much less committed a crime.

This couldn't be happening.

The elevator doors opened and she was suddenly inside, moving downward. The sensation of falling had her stomach rushing up into her already clogged throat.

Grabbing for the wall she struggled to adjust her equilibrium.

"You okay?"

An arm went around her waist in the nick of time.

Mary Jane had never fainted in her life, but she was suddenly certain that was exactly what she was going to do. In an elevator in front of a virtual stranger.

"Thank you. I'm…I'm okay." She tried to steady herself. To move away from his overpowering nearness but she couldn't. She wasn't all right. She was anything but. Everything she'd thought about the events of one year ago was suddenly in question.

"Some sleep will do you good," he offered, his deep voice uncharacteristically gentle. "You're exhausted and you've had two major shocks in less than twenty-four hours. You've every right to be unsettled."

He was right. Darn it.

Mary Jane closed her eyes to hold back the flood of tumultuous emotion. She tried so hard to hold her own, to stay strong but couldn't. She surrendered and leaned into the support his broad shoulder offered.

What had her sister been thinking? Leaving this kind of mess for her?

A sob caught in her throat. But what if this wasn't her sister's doing? What if Rebecca was dead? This could be some kind of game to prompt results. Some twisted plan to accomplish some sick goal. If someone thought she had information or evidence her sister had given her, they would stop at nothing to get their hands on it. Mind games would only be the beginning.

Mary Jane stopped fighting the internal battle and

let the emotions rock through her. Some part of her recognized that the elevator had stopped moving without reaching its destination and that Shane Allen's arms were around her, enveloping her completely.

She appreciated the silence…appreciated his strength. He didn't make her any promises he might not be able to keep. He just held her. Let her cry the way she needed to.

Seconds or maybe minutes passed before the wave of shuddering emotion passed. The receding fervor left behind the heat of embarrassment. God, she hadn't cried like this in ages. During her parents' illness she'd been stoic. Even as she'd said her final good-byes at the cemetery she'd maintained her composure.

Mary Jane swiped her cheeks with the backs of her hands and tried to prod a smile into place. "Sorry. I…" She moistened her lips and decided there was no explanation. Nothing she could say to explain away the weakness she'd just displayed. She was tired of being strong. *Damned* tired.

As if he understood her inability to articulate what she felt, he let the conversation lapse and leaned past her, pressed the button for the basement garage and set the car back into motion.

She turned to face the gleaming stainless steel doors and wondered how it was that a man who rode such a bad-boy machine, wore mostly leather and denim, and who made no excuses for his long hair or his whiskered chin could be so perceptive and compassionate.

Just went to show that the adage you couldn't judge a book by its cover was certainly true. All this time she'd considered herself above passing judgment. He wasn't the cliché, she was.

The elevator glided to a stop, and the doors parted. She stepped out. He followed. She would be glad to get home. She was tired. Tired and totally drained. The idea that the bashed skull she had imagined might belong to someone who had actually sold herself to that fate kept gnawing at her insides. What was wrong with this world that desperation could push a person to that point?

"Would you like something to eat?" he asked as they neared her car. "I could take a detour through a drive-through or convenience store. Get sandwiches. Soup. Something easy."

Good grief. She hadn't eaten all day. No wonder she was wobbling on her feet. And this poor man. She'd had him in her home and hadn't offered him anything to eat or drink. She really was out of it.

But then she had an excuse. She'd spent so little time at her place the past few months she rarely bothered with shopping. Bottled water and crackers wouldn't likely do the job.

"That would be nice." She had no idea what he would find open at this hour but maybe he knew more about that than she did. She was never out at this time of night. "I'm afraid my cupboards are pretty bare."

He paused, his hand on the passenger side door and then he smiled. Maybe the fainting episode hadn't passed. She felt light-headed. Probably her blood sugar level had bottomed out. Whatever the case, she was pretty sure she'd never seen a smile quite so…genuinely nice. The streetlamp spot-lighted straight, white teeth. Generous lips. And a sparkle in those dark eyes that reflected just how deeply the smile went.

"I know all about bare cupboards. Mine usually stay that way. Seems a waste to stock up for *one*."

The amusement in his expression vanished and was instantly replaced by a distant sadness.

One. He was alone. Like her. His wife had cheated on him. Had left him when he was already down for the count. What kind of person did that?

Perhaps the two of them had far more in common than she had first thought.

He opened the car door and the moment passed. She settled into the seat. He closed the door. She watched as he rounded the hood. What would it be like to live with a man like him? To feel protected by his strength. She'd never had that…never had time.

She stared, couldn't help herself, as he slid behind the steering wheel. Would he be a loving husband and father beneath that roguish exterior? Was the woman who'd walked out on him looking for the polished elegance he hadn't been able to give her? Or had he once been those things and had changed and she no longer wanted him?

Sleep. Mary Jane really, really needed sleep. She was obsessing on the most bizarre subjects.

He turned his head and his dark brown eyes locked with hers. "Is there a question coming or is this analysis going to be the silent type?"

The fire of humiliation roared up her neck and over her cheeks. She was pretty sure even the roots of her red hair blazed a little redder.

"I'm sorry." She forced her attention front and center. "I'm tired. I'm obsessing."

God, why didn't he just let it go? Instead, he stared at her the way she obviously had him. Waiting for her to speak her mind.

Might as well get it over with.

"I just wondered…" How did she ask this? He'd been so nice to her. What the heck? Tonight had definitely been a night of bizarre events. What was one more? "When you were a marshal…did you…" She gestured helplessly. "You don't dress like the others. The suit. The whole polished image."

The light filtering through the windshield was reflected by the intensity in his eyes. "I worked deep-cover operations. I couldn't afford to look like a marshal. Fading into the background was important. But I wore the requisite suit when necessary. More often than I wanted to."

The sound that bubbled out of her throat might have passed for laughter had she been a little more enthusiastic. "I'm sorry. I can't imagine you fading into the background."

"You'd be surprised what I can do when the need arises."

That she didn't doubt for a second.

He started the engine, checked the mirror and pulled away from the curb without further elaboration.

Mary Jane closed her eyes and relaxed into her seat. Tomorrow would be better. It had to be. There were too many questions and not nearly enough answers.

The jingle of her cell phone shattered the peaceful silence and made her heart thud. She reached for her purse and fished around for her phone. It was a miracle it still worked considering she'd forgotten to charge it at any point during the past forty-eight hours.

She frowned at the display. *Unknown caller.* She didn't get that many calls, and those she did, she generally recognized. "Hello?"

"MJ?"

Everything inside Mary Jane stilled. Even her heart seemed to stutter. "Rebecca?"

Impossible.

Her sister was dead...wasn't she?

"Don't trust anyone," the familiar voice warned.

Glass shattered and the car swerved.

"Get down!" Investigator Allen shouted.

Before Mary Jane could react, the window next to her burst and fragments of glass sprayed across her chest...across her lap.

Someone was shooting at them.

"Get down!" Allen grabbed her by the back of the head and shoved her downward.

Someone was shooting at them.

Chapter Seven

Shane swerved into the left lane and made a hard turn. The instant the rear wheels were back in line with the front, he slammed his foot down on the accelerator.

A glance in the rearview mirror told him they were still coming.

At least two perps. The driver and a front-seat passenger. One weapon doing all the firing.

"What's happening?"

"Stay down!" He pushed the sedan harder. The vehicle on his tail was a muscle car, lots of horses under the hood. A hell of a lot more than this meek midsize economy job.

A shot pierced the rear window.

Mary Jane screamed.

Evasive maneuver to the right. Then left.

Even at a speed of nearly one hundred miles per hour, Shane took his right hand off the wheel to reach for his cell phone.

Another shot finished shattering the rear window.

Glass spewed. Heat tore through his left forearm. He dropped the cell. Grabbed the steering wheel with his right hand as pain roared down his left arm.

He was hit.

Damn it.

Mary Jane fumbled around in the floorboard. He couldn't take his eyes off the street as he darted right, then left…and repeated, then reversed. Whatever she was doing, as long as she stayed down, she would be okay.

"I'm…calling 9-1-1," she said, her voice high-pitched and broken. Evidently she'd retrieved the phone he'd dropped or had dug out her own.

The sudden throb of blue lights in the rearview mirror sent relief searing through him.

"Don't bother. They're here."

He slammed on the brakes and slid to the curb. Shoved the vehicle into Park and threw his upper body across his passenger as the predator whizzed by.

A final shot cracked the windshield.

Mary Jane shrieked.

The sound of a car lurching to a stop next to them had Shane reaching for his weapon.

"Hands in the air where I can see them!"

A cop.

The harsh glare from his flashlight hit Shane in the face.

"Now!" the cop shouted.

Shane groaned as he lifted his hands above his

head. The warm liquid seeping beneath the sleeve of his jacket warned that he needed medical attention, punctuating the announcement the pain had screamed loudly and clearly already.

The passenger-side door opened. "Out of the car, ma'am! Slow and easy."

"It'll be all right," Shane offered, hoping to reassure her with his eyes. Hers were wide with fear, but she nodded her understanding. He'd decided that the lady was a lot tougher than she looked.

"Get out of the vehicle, pal," the cop on his side of the car ordered as the door was yanked open. "No sudden moves."

Shane kept his hands high as he dropped his boots to the pavement and pushed out of the car. He swallowed the groan that accompanied the brushing of his arm against the doorframe as he made the move. "I'm carrying a Glock nine millimeter in my shoulder holster." This wasn't the time for surprises. Full disclosure meant no unnecessary excitement.

He winced as the cop reached beneath his jacket and retrieved the weapon.

"Are you injured?" The officer surveyed him cautiously as he secured the confiscated weapon.

"I am. Left bicep. There's ID in my wallet," Shane added. "I'm an investigator for the Colby Agency."

The radio on the officer's hip crackled. "We lost 'em," someone's voice rattled off.

"That car," Shane said with a nod to the radio,

"attacked us as we were leaving a meeting with my employer, Victoria Colby-Camp." He tossed the Colby name in as often as possible since Chicago PD held the agency in such high regard.

"We'll sort this out at the precinct," the cop said without a hint of sympathy. "Assume the position."

Shane faced the car he'd exited, braced his hands atop it and spread his legs. He couldn't really blame the cop. A shoot-out at midnight in downtown Chicago wasn't exactly the sort of thing one dismissed so easily.

As soon as the boys in blue figured out Shane was one of the good guys, all would be cool.

MARY JANE HAD NEVER BEEN SO humiliated in her life as she was when the police officer patted her down, then cuffed her hands behind her back.

"We're the victims," she told him for the tenth time. Why wasn't he listening?

"This way, ma'am," he ordered as he ushered her around the rear of her car and toward the official vehicle waiting on the other side.

Shane had been cuffed in the same manner and was about to climb into the backseat of the squad car when Mary Jane saw the blood dripping from his left hand. A shriek rent the air. It wasn't until the sound had stopped echoing in the night that she realized it had come from her.

Both officers and Shane stared at her.

"He's bleeding," she snapped, worry and frustration overriding the fear she had felt. "He needs medical attention. Are you going to ignore that? Isn't there a law against that?" She looked from the officer clutching Shane's right arm to the man manacling hers.

Two more squad cars arrived just then.

There was some discussion before it was decided that a trip to Mercy General was in order prior to hauling them in to be questioned.

"Thank God," she muttered as she was guided into the backseat of the squad car belonging to the first officers on the scene. The door slammed and she flinched at the sound. She was tired and her nerves were shot. A shudder shook her hard. It wasn't until the warmth inside the car had invaded her senses that she realized how cold she'd gotten standing out there. It was freezing.

Raised voices had her gaze swinging toward the other door where Shane still stood outside. Two officers were arguing with him.

"I go where she goes," he countered whatever had been said. "I'm her bodyguard."

Bodyguard? A frown tugged at her forehead. She supposed that was true. He'd certainly kept her from getting shot a few minutes ago.

If he hadn't evaded the trouble…hadn't forced her down into the seat…she shuddered as the possibilities flashed through her mind.

The heated exchange escalated, and Detective Bailen's name was tossed around before Shane was finally allowed to get into the backseat with her. Good thing he thought to mention Bailen. She should have.

Relief made her head swim. Thank God. She really needed this day to be over. And she much preferred that he was close by…this stranger she'd suddenly come to depend on.

The officer and his partner got into the front and headed for the hospital. The driver spoke into the radio, giving the dispatcher an update, while the other made notes on the police report on his clipboard.

"You okay?"

Her attention shifted to the man next to her. "Am I okay?" Was he insane? They'd been shot at. He was bleeding. Her car was trashed. And she was handcuffed in the back of a police car.

"No," she said, hysterical laughter fizzing into her throat. "I'm definitely not okay."

"It's pretty scary the first time."

Her gaze collided with his again. "The first time?"

"The first time you get shot at," he clarified.

She suddenly wondered how he could sit there and speak so calmly and quietly when he was bleeding. He'd been injured by a bullet from a shooter who had obviously been trying to kill them.

Someone had tried to kill them…because of her…or something they thought she knew or possessed.

And she…she was crying.

"Damn it." She scrubbed first one cheek then the other against her shoulders. She hadn't even realized the tears had started. What was wrong with her? It wasn't like she was the one bleeding.

Then she remembered the call.

"It was her," she blurted. At his questioning look, she explained, "Rebecca. She called my cell phone right before those…*people* started shooting at us."

"You're sure it was her?"

Was she sure? Her sister was supposed to be dead. She'd vanished eleven months ago. Her remains had been identified. Or maybe not. Was it her sister on the phone? Could she be absolutely certain?

No, she couldn't be sure it was *her*…but it was definitely her voice.

"I'd know her voice anywhere. The voice was hers." The words could have been from some kind of recording done before she died…if she was dead.

If. If. *If.*

Mary Jane dropped her head against the seat and closed her eyes. Dear God, what had her sister gotten her into? The tire on her car had been slashed. Her apartment searched. And now this. Her car was riddled with bullet holes. She'd seen a couple of holes in the metal, not to mention all the broken windows.

At least she understood exactly what Victoria Colby-Camp had been talking about when she'd mentioned the dangers of shadowing an investigator.

But this was her sister's mess.

Her mess.

And this man had nearly lost his life.

More of those confounding tears rolled down her cheeks and she had to look away—look at anything except the man next to her. Her need to have the truth could have cost him his life.

"Rebecca," she murmured, "what have you done?"

THE DOCTOR WASN'T HAPPY ABOUT the crowded room, but he would just have to deal with it. Shane wasn't letting Mary Jane out of his sight and Officer Woody wasn't allowing Shane out of his presence. With the nurse, that made five people in the small exam room. And Woody's partner was in the corridor just outside the door.

Detective Bailen was on his way, as was Simon Ruhl.

A real party.

"It's a soft tissue wound," the doctor confirmed. "Clear entrance and exit wounds. Not too serious but fairly deep." He looked over his wire-rimmed glasses at Shane. "You're sure you don't want something besides the local for the pain?"

Shane moved his head side to side. "Just do it."

He fixed his attention on Mary Jane as the doctor began. The first prick made him wince, but after that he was good. Mary Jane's hands shook as she shoved long, silky strands of fiery red hair behind her ears. Her skin was as pale as porcelain and looked every bit as smooth. He hadn't noticed until then the sprinkling of freckles across her nose. Went with the territory of being a fair-skinned redhead, he supposed.

Her sister had said in her video message that no one should die a virgin. He wondered if, these days, a twenty-nine-year-old woman who hadn't been living in a cave could actually be a virgin. Maybe Rebecca just hadn't been privy to her sister's private life.

Those wide blue eyes locked on his, and he hoped Mary Jane couldn't read his mind and that she wasn't going to cry again. She'd proven pretty damned strong so far, considering what she'd been through. But he couldn't tolerate those tears.

He never could.

His ex had used the power of tears to make him feel guilty for her mistakes so many times. If she blew the budget, he felt guilty. If she forgot Matt's play dates, it was Shane's fault. She never took responsibility for anything. Not even for cheating with his best friend.

Fury twisted his gut. He was a fool to be going down that path again.

He'd been one then and evidently he hadn't learned his lesson yet. Otherwise this woman wouldn't have him wishing he could dry those tears dampening her cheeks.

Keeping her safe while getting to the bottom of

what happened to her sister was his job. Keeping her happy wasn't. He had to remember that.

"That's got it." The doctor stepped back and let the nurse take care of the dressing.

As the doctor left the exam room to move on to his next patient, the officer in the corridor stuck his head inside. "Woody, Detective Bailen from Homicide is here, and he needs to speak with you."

Good. That was going to save Shane a lot of explaining. Between Bailen and Ruhl, they should be able to clear up the incident. Shane really wanted to get this woman home.

Problem was, he couldn't risk taking her back to her own place. And there was the detail of his Harley at her place. Simon could take care of that problem. But convincing Mary Jane to go home with him might prove considerably more of an issue.

"You'll need to pick up your follow-up orders at the desk," the nurse told him as she finished dressing the sutured wound.

The door opened and a suit walked in. Before Shane could decide if he was FBI or the Marshals, the man flashed his credentials.

"Special Agent John LeMire."

Now the real fun began.

"Will you excuse us, ma'am," the agent said to the nurse. His navy suit looked fresh from the cleaners, not a single crease. He appeared to be about forty, with a hint of gray at his dark temples.

The nurse gave the agent a tight smile, took her tray and exited the room.

"Ms. Brooks, I hope you're all right," LeMire said to Mary Jane.

"I'm fine."

The way her arms were hugged around her middle didn't back up her assertion. Shane knew she wasn't all right. Far from it.

LeMire's interest focused on Shane once more. "I was unaware a private investigation firm was involved in the Rebecca Brooks case."

"Detective Bailen should have kept you up to speed," Shane countered as he slid off the exam table and reached for his damaged jacket. "He was fully aware of Ms. Brooks's decision to retain our services." He gritted his teeth as he pulled on the leather coat that had been his favorite for a hell of a long time. He doubted it would be so easy to repair this time.

"I'm sure you're aware that you are legally obligated to share any information or evidence you discover with the Bureau."

"Yep." He adjusted his jacket and tried to ignore the ache in his arm with each movement. "I assured Bailen that I understood my responsibilities." He let go a big breath, hoping to exhale some of the frustration and fatigue, as well. Didn't work. "Any more questions?"

"This is a very sensitive case," LeMire countered. "I'm concerned that your agency's tampering may damage our efforts to reorganize our case against Horizon Software."

Shane appreciated his frankness. "The way I understand it, you don't have a case without a key witness." He moved toward Mary Jane. "If there's nothing else, we're ready to go now."

LeMire pointed an accusing finger at him. "We'll be watching you, Allen. I know more about you than you know about yourself. Don't think we're unaware of the grudge you have against Marshal Mitchell, as well as those who made the decision to retire you."

Shane allowed one corner of his mouth to tilt upward. "You know how to reach me." He guided Mary Jane out of the room. He wasn't going to be pressured by these guys. He had a job to do and he was well aware of the rules of discovery and disclosure. As far as grudges went, he didn't waste the energy. Though he couldn't deny despising Mitchell's existence when forced to interact with the bastard. He was only human after all.

In the corridor Detective Bailen, Simon Ruhl and another fed waited, and judging by their stern expressions no one was happy.

"You okay?" Ruhl asked.

Shane laughed softly at all the attention. He couldn't remember when he'd had this many people concerned about his well-being. "Just a scratch."

Ruhl nodded. "I'll update Victoria."

Victoria Colby-Camp wouldn't rest until she knew her people were safe. That was the thing about the Colby Agency. It wasn't like joining a staff, it was more like becoming a part of a special club…a family.

"Officer Woody has been brought up to speed," Bailen said, "on the situation. His report will reflect that you and Ms. Brooks were the victims of a drive-by shooting."

What else could they say at this point?

"You didn't get a look at the unknown subjects?" LeMire's partner, Agent Richard Farmer, wanted to know.

Shane shook his head. "I was a little busy avoiding gunfire." He looked to Bailen. "The cops should have a license plate number."

"Dead end," Bailen told him. "The car was stolen. Found it a few blocks from the scene. We'll, of course, have the forensics techs go over the vehicle for any prints or trace evidence."

And they would get nothing. "These guys were professionals," Shane warned. "I don't think they intended to kill anyone. I'd wager that this was a scare tactic."

"Well, it worked," Mary Jane muttered.

Ruhl looked from Mary Jane to Shane. "Time to move to the next level," he suggested.

Shane nodded. He'd already decided that. He

gave Ruhl the key to his Harley. "Could you have someone deliver her for me?"

Ruhl nodded. "A car is waiting whenever you're ready."

"Wait." Bailen's expression was furrowed with confusion. "How can you be sure this was just a scare tactic?"

"I'd like to hear the answer to that one myself," LeMire added smugly.

"They were on our tail for three or four minutes," Shane explained. "I executed evasive maneuvers, but they had the advantage from the get-go. The shots were placed wide. I think this—" he moved his left arm slightly "—was a ricochet, not a direct hit." Of course he couldn't be certain, but instinct told him that during those minutes of high-speed chase the passenger had had ample opportunity to attain a headshot. Shane had been a visible target the entire time. If the intent had been to kill him, he would be dead now.

Bailen shoved back his lapels and planted his hands on his hips. "The trouble appears to have started with your interference," he said to Shane. "I'm not sure Ms. Brooks understands how much danger she might very well be in while in your company."

"The trouble," Shane countered, "started when your department released the announcement that the remains of a star witness in a federal case had been identified."

The official authorities in the group all started to talk at once then. Ruhl and Shane exchanged a glance. The involvement of multiple agencies always made for awkward moments like this. There was always lots of accusations and no one willing to accept responsibility.

Shane leaned toward Mary Jane. "Let's get out of here."

They made a simultaneous about-face and headed for the exit to the lobby. Bailen and LeMire shouted after them, but Shane didn't look back. The sound of Simon Ruhl's commanding voice interrupted whatever opposition the men would have launched next, giving Shane and Mary Jane just enough time to escape through the Authorized Personnel Only doors.

Shane didn't slow until they'd reached the exit to the parking lot. The sooner they were out of here and at his place the better.

Mary Jane hesitated at the curb. "What're we going to do now?"

He spotted the car, complete with driver. "The agency's provided transportation. We'll—"

"Allen, you're in over your head."

Shane's gaze swung toward the man striding toward them. Derrick Mitchell. Fury instantly ignited in Shane's gut. What the hell did he want now?

"Ms. Brooks," Mitchell said as he reached their position. "I would strongly advise you to reconsider working with this man. He's a loose cannon. If you're counting on him taking care of you, then you should talk to the last person who counted on him. And that would be me."

Shane didn't remember throwing the punch, but he knew exactly when his fist connected with the bastard's jaw. Mitchell staggered back a couple of steps.

Dan Bolton stepped between them in time to cut off the next swing. "That's enough," he ordered, looking from one to the other.

"I could charge you with assault," Mitchell threatened.

"So do it," Shane goaded. Let him. Landing that punch was worth an assault charge.

"No one will be charging anyone with anything," Bolton growled. "You asked for that one, Mitchell."

Mary Jane tugged at Shane's sleeve. "Let's go."

He felt exactly like an ass when he got a look at her expression. She was exhausted and frightened and he'd taken the bait and ended up in a fight.

Shane headed for the car, his hand resting against the small of her back. His full attention had to be one place only: protecting this woman from whatever demons her sister had left behind.

Chapter Eight

"Thanks, man."

Shane slapped the top of the car and it rolled away. Mary Jane's gaze moved from the taillights disappearing down the street to the small house sitting on a postage stamp-size lawn.

Craftsman-style bungalow. The streetlamp on the corner chased the shadows from the yard onto the porch. The neighborhood was quiet save for a dog barking three houses away. Apparently their arrival had awakened him from his sleep.

There were about a dozen questions she wanted to ask as Shane ushered her up the walk to the steps, but she was too busy attempting to see the details through the darkness.

He unlocked the door, reached inside and flipped a switch, then waited for her to go inside first. Three steps and one deep breath later and she knew for sure she was in his home. It smelled like him, like leather and earthy spices.

The click of the latch and a chain sliding into place echoed behind her as he secured the door. She gasped as something brushed her leg. Then she smiled as a big gray cat rubbed against her again.

"That's Gypsy," he told her as he tossed the keys onto a table by the door.

Mary Jane crouched down to smooth her hand over the sleek fur. "Gypsy?"

"Yeah." He shouldered out of his jacket, wincing twice as he did so. "She wanders like a tomcat. But she always comes back."

Mary Jane scooped the cat into her arms, the sound of its rhythmic purring soothing. "Are we here to get you a change of clothes?" They really hadn't talked much on the way over. She had assumed that he didn't want to talk about the case in front of the driver. Her excuse was far more selfish—she'd been exhausted.

But—she turned all the way around to take a look at the living room—now that she was here she'd gotten her second wind, which was mainly boosted by her curiosity. How did a guy who rode a Harley live?

Things looked pretty normal so far. Comfortable sectional sofa in a deep forest green. Heavy wood tables and a massive television—one of the flat-panel types mounted on the wall. Probably surround sound and all that guy stuff.

"Why don't I see what I can pull together in the kitchen?"

Her stomach rumbled at the suggestion. "I could eat," she admitted. As if understanding that food was about to be prepared, Gypsy struggled to get free. Mary Jane set her down on the floor and then watched as she followed her master into the kitchen.

The kitchen was nearly as large as the living room. The cabinets and appliances circled the room, leaving a table and chairs as the centerpiece. More of that dark, heavy wood with a butcher block countertop. Neat, clean. She doubted he did a lot of cooking. In fact, he'd said something about his cupboards being bare most of the time, too.

She shoved her hair behind her ear, and something caught between her fingers. She peered at the object. Glass. Good grief. She hadn't thought of checking her hair for debris.

"Could I use your bathroom?" She also hadn't considered that she likely looked a fright.

"Sure." He sat a skillet on the stovetop. "Down the hall, first door on the left."

She returned to the living room and took the only other doorway, which led into the hall. Two doors on each side. Home office on the right, then a bedroom. Probably a guest room. She didn't see any sign of her host in that room. Directly across the hall was his room. The bed was unmade, but otherwise it was fairly neat.

As much as she wanted to linger, she made her way to the final door, the bathroom. A groan vibrated in her throat as she caught sight of her reflection. "What a wreck." After searching the drawers in the vanity, she settled on a comb. No brush. This would take some time. Slowly, she detangled the wild mass. Several fragments of glass dropped onto the white-tiled counter.

She washed her face and hands and straightened her clothes. The blouse had held up pretty well, but her skirt was wrinkled and had a small snag in the material on her right hip. She had no idea how she'd managed that, but considering she'd been chased and shot at, she couldn't really complain.

For a minute or two she stared at her reflection. At the same blue eyes as her sister's. Was it possible Rebecca could still be alive?

As much as she wanted that to be true, Mary Jane wasn't sure she could ever hope to understand how this all happened if that were the case. But maybe she wasn't being fair. She didn't have all the facts. She had no idea what her sister had been through or why she had done whatever it was she'd done.

For now, she had to give Rebecca the benefit of the doubt.

She went back to the kitchen and found Shane scraping scrambled eggs onto plates. He looked up, smiled.

"I'm not much of a cook, but I can do eggs and toast."

Her mouth watered. She really was hungry. "Smells heavenly."

"Have a seat." He set the skillet in the sink. "I'll get the toast and the beer."

Beer?

Two slices of browned bread popped from the toaster. He placed them on a plate and set the plate on the table between the two already laded with scrambled eggs. Then he reached into the fridge and withdrew two longneck bottles of cold beer.

Beer.

Well, there was a first time for everything.

"Would you like a glass?" He deposited an open bottle in front of her.

"Do you use a glass?"

He shook his head, another smile slid across his lips. "You don't drink beer, do you?"

Her mother had always taught her to pretend she liked whatever was served to her when a guest in someone else's home. To do otherwise was rude, in her mother's esteemed opinion.

"Who doesn't?" she tossed back, determined to be a sport considering what he'd gone through tonight to protect her.

The smile stretched into a grin as he opened the second bottle and took his seat. "Eat," he encouraged. "We'll both feel a lot better when we've gotten some fuel into us."

"How long have you lived here?" she asked as

she lifted a forkful of eggs to her mouth. Her lips closed around the tines and she had to close her eyes at the ecstasy.

"Just over a year."

She moaned, startling herself. The eggs were so, so good.

"Milk and butter are the keys," he offered as he scooped up a forkful himself.

She was certain she'd never had eggs that tasted this good. Fluffy, buttery. "Wow." She forgot all about the rest of her questions and focused on consuming the eggs and toast. She barely noticed the beer's bitter tang.

When she'd taken the last bite, she sighed wistfully. As silly as it sounded, she could have eaten more.

The roar she'd come to recognize as the sound of his motorcycle radiated through the quiet house.

"Let me take care of this." He stood. "You stay put." He nodded to her bottle. "Finish your beer."

She supposed one of his colleagues had delivered the motorcycle he'd left at her home. That was a good thing, considering they wouldn't have any transportation otherwise. Not that she would be climbing astride that monstrous cycle. She shivered at the thought. She would need a rental until her car was repaired.

Fatigue swamped her again as she finished off her beer. How was she getting home? Right now she could lay her head down just about anywhere and sleep like a baby.

But first, someone had to do these dishes. She pushed back her chair and set to the task. Most everything except the skillet could be loaded into the dishwasher. Five minutes max. If he cooked, the least she could do was clean up.

She'd just finished wiping down the stove and drying the freshly washed skillet when Shane came back inside. The idea that she was calling him by his first name occurred to her. Somewhere amid the flying bullets or just prior to that event, she'd started thinking of him as Shane rather than Investigator Allen.

That was normal. A man who'd risked his life for hers was certainly one she could call by his first name.

"You didn't have to clean up."

She tossed the towel aside. "It was a breeze." The questions she needed to ask filtered back into her mind. "Are we going to my house now?" She sure hoped he had a car out there in addition to his motorcycle. As much as she wanted to go home, she didn't want to go that badly. She felt a little lightheaded. The beer probably.

"We need to talk about that." He indicated the living room. "Let's take a load off and discuss our options."

She followed him into the living room and made herself comfortable on one end of the oversized sectional sofa. After smoothing her skirt as best she could, she relaxed into the full cushions. She felt warm and content, even if she was in a strange place.

"I don't think it's safe to go back to your place," he said right off the bat.

Some sort of plan to evade trouble was expected. But she couldn't say she'd anticipated not being able to go back home.

"Are we going to a hotel or a safe house?" She'd heard about those in the movies.

He settled deeper into the cushions on the opposite end of the sofa. "We'll be fine here for now."

Okay, she was tired, that was true. But she really should have seen that one coming.

"Oh." How did she feel about that? "Okay." She'd seen the guest room…right across the hall from his bedroom. She could deal with that…couldn't she?

"Tomorrow," he began, but then amended, "today, actually, after we've had some rest, we'll start looking into Jason Mackey and see if we can make a connection between him and Amanda Ferguson. We'll also try and track down any family she may have had."

Sounded like the best way to proceed. She closed her eyes and replayed the voice on the cell phone. Definitely her sister's voice.

But what did that mean?

"I have a shirt you can sleep in."

Mary Jane's eyes fluttered open. The idea of sleeping in anything that belonged to him unsettled her. But the thought of sleeping in her clothes was far too unappealing to dismiss his suggestion.

"I think I'm ready to call it a night." She had more questions, but she was just too tired to push for answers. And, frankly, she didn't want to be alone in the same room with him anymore.

There was one question she really needed an answer to but she hated to ask. Yet, he was responsible for her safety. She had a right to know about the outburst outside the hospital.

"I'll show you to the guest room." He settled his hands on his knees and prepared to get up.

"I do have one question," she said, waylaying his intention.

"What's that?"

"What's the story between you and Marshal Mitchell?" Whatever it was, it wasn't pretty.

Any hint of the smiles she'd seen moments ago vanished. The somber expression that claimed his face made her regret having asked.

"He was my partner," Shane told her. "He stole my wife and my career." With that, he stood.

His posture as well as his expression warned that he wasn't entertaining any more questions.

Mary Jane got to her feet and followed him into the hall. He left her in the guest room long enough to get one of his shirts.

"If you need anything I'll be right across the hall." He offered the shirt.

"Thank you." Mary Jane accepted the shirt.

Her host walked out of the room. Instead of going into his room he went to the bedroom turned office. Since he didn't bother with a good-night, she didn't, either.

She could certainly understand his hesitation to talk about the past. What kind of partner stole another man's wife? The part about his career wasn't clear. Instinct told her it had something to do with his shooting. She hugged the shirt he'd given her close to her chest. All that made for a major chip to be carried around. She wondered if he still loved the woman he'd been married to at the time.

An automated voice echoed in the hall. "*You have one new message.*"

"*Mr. Allen, this is Harry Rosen. I'm calling to inform you that the judge has declined your petition for a hearing on visitation rights. You'll have no choice but to obtain counsel and proceed to court if you still want to pursue visitation rights. Think about it long and hard, Mr. Allen. It's a battle you can't possibly hope to win.*"

"*Message deleted.*"

"*End of messages.*"

Before she had the presence of mind to close her door, he had stepped from the office and headed to his own room across the hall.

Their gazes collided.

"Sorry," she muttered. "I didn't mean to eavesdrop." Good heavens. What had she been thinking?

"Just something else I have to thank Mitchell for," he said coldly before going into his room.

No wonder he was bitter. Somehow, his ex-wife was preventing him from seeing his child. That had to be terribly painful.

She blinked when she realized he was shedding his clothes. The pullover sweater hit the floor first. Then the T-shirt.

He looked lean with his clothes on, but bare, there were plenty of rippling muscles. The white bandage was stark against his darker skin. When he sat down on the edge of the bed to remove his boots, their gazes connected across the hall.

She jumped.

He stared.

"Is there something else you want to know, Ms. Brooks?"

No. She told herself to say no.

Before the message penetrated her brain she was standing at his door. "You have a child?"

He tossed aside the first boot, then pulled off the other. "A stepson."

"Did you adopt him?" The scent of him was invading her lungs and making her feel light-headed again. Or maybe it was the beer or the exhaustion.

"Not legally." He stood, reached for his belt. "But that doesn't mean I don't love him."

Leather hissing against denim drew her attention to the belt sliding free of his jeans. And then her gaze traveled upward, to that ribbed abdomen. Her throat went dry.

"I'm…sorry." She met his eyes once more. "That must be hard." She'd given up on the idea of ever having any children. Loving one and then losing him had to be a nightmare.

He took a step toward her. "So am I."

Another step disappeared between them.

"I'm taking the issue to court."

"Oh."

He stood directly in front of her now.

"I'm not giving up without a fight."

She moistened her lips, tried to swallow. There was something about the way he towered over her, that dark silky hair touching his broad shoulders. The essence of hot male skin drifting into her nostrils. Her head was spinning.

"Good for you."

"You should go to bed now, Ms. Brooks."

There was nothing in his words that should have had heat stirring inside her, but the fire ignited deep in her belly from the intensity in his eyes. He was warning her…and inviting her at the same time.

"I shouldn't be in danger," she offered, unable to just turn away. "I don't know anything. This is all a mistake…or something…"

"You are in danger, Ms. Brooks," he cautioned,

his voice lower now. As she watched, his gaze dropped to her mouth but only for a moment. "I'll get to the bottom of the reason why, but right now we both need sleep."

She nodded. "I'm not afraid." She wasn't. Not really. She'd been afraid in the car going more than a hundred miles per hour and bullets flying. But she wasn't afraid now. She wanted the truth. Whatever it took to find it, she wanted it.

He searched her eyes as if he were looking for something in particular that he wasn't finding. The tension inched up her spine with every passing second, sending heat outward, along her limbs, beyond her belly into her deepest feminine recesses. She didn't remember the last time she'd had a reaction like this to a man. Years.

"Good night, Ms. Brooks."

He turned and walked back into his room. Still wearing his jeans, he climbed into his bed. She didn't move away from the door until he'd turned out the lamp next to his bed.

She didn't bother with the light in her room. She stripped off her clothes and pulled on his shirt. The smell of him immediately enveloped her. She pulled back the covers of the bed and climbed beneath them. One deep breath after the other. She wanted to fill her lungs with the courage his scent offered.

For the first time in a long time she felt as if she wasn't so alone.

Chapter Nine

At 8:00 a.m. sharp the knock came at Shane's door.

Simon Ruhl had arrived with a dossier on Jason Mackey and a bag of essential items from Mary Jane's home.

"Coffee?" Shane asked as he accepted the file.

"No, thanks." Ruhl set the overnight bag on the floor and glanced around the living room. "How is Ms. Brooks this morning?"

Shane glanced toward the hall. "Still asleep. Yesterday wasn't exactly a normal day in her life." Not by any stretch of the imagination. Mary Jane Brooks was a quiet, conservative school teacher who took care of the ill and needy. A regular Florence Nightingale. The kind of woman who represented wholesome living and selfless giving. And still, she'd kept him from sleeping last night. Not a single thing about the ideas that churned in his brain had been wholesome or selfless. Mostly they'd been about getting so deep inside her that their bodies would be like one.

Ruhl gestured to the bag at his feet. "Nicole assembled the essentials as well as changes of clothes and the cell phone charger she found on the kitchen counter at Ms. Brooks's home."

Nicole was Ian Michaels's wife and a fellow Colby Agency investigator.

"Sounds like everything we'll need."

"Ben has tied a link to her cell number. Any calls that come in will be traced and recorded on our end without interruption to her. Ben has a friend who can do a voice analysis in the event she receives another call she believes to be from her sister."

"Excellent." Shane gestured to the sofa before heading that way. "She's convinced the voice was Rebecca's," he said as he sat down and opened the file on Jason Mackey.

"It could very well have been her sister's voice," Ruhl agreed. "We both know that with today's technology most anything is possible, especially if one has access to recordings of a person's voice."

That was the thing. Shane leveled his gaze on Ruhl. "We also know that every interview conducted with her Bureau contacts and with the marshals who would oversee her transfer into Witness Security would have been recorded." Shane would be the first to admit that he would like nothing better than to pin this on his former partner, the bastard. But even he realized that was a long shot. Just because the guy was a complete jerk didn't mean he was a killer or dirty.

"Conference calls, meetings, any number of activities at Horizon Software may have been recorded as well," Ruhl offered. "This may be someone from that side of this ugly game. If she left behind something that could incriminate them, they would certainly want to find it."

"But why wait all this time?" Shane returned, playing devil's advocate. "Why not months ago? Horizon Software snubbed its nose at the feds after she disappeared. From what I've read, the CEO has carried on as if the whole investigation never happened. Now, suddenly, with the announcement that her remains have been identified, her only living relative is being shot at and receiving warnings from beyond the grave. What changed other than official confirmation, as far as anyone else knows, that Rebecca Brooks is dead?"

"That's the million-dollar question," Ruhl agreed. "Victoria has Ian monitoring Horizon Software activities, particularly Anthony Chambers, the CEO. Ann Martin is keeping an eye on Ms. Brooks's apartment. Ben is monitoring the landline there, as well."

"Sounds like we have everything covered." That was one of the things Shane enjoyed about working at the Colby Agency. Nothing was ever left to chance. The Colby Agency was the best and employed only the best. Like Ben Haygood and Ann Martin. Ann was fairly new, like Shane. She had been an electronic banking specialist before coming on board as a Colby Agency investigator.

Ruhl pointed to the file Shane had spread out before him. "I've read over his dossier," he said. "Mackey doesn't sound like such a bad guy, but he had friends who were the worst of the worst. Not to mention he was a distant cousin to Anthony Chambers. Be careful treading into that territory."

Shane appreciated the advice, but he knew how to handle himself in the field. "Do we know anything else on Amanda Ferguson?"

"Nicole is working with an FBI contact on the lists that Ben discovered. I'll keep you posted on her progress." Ruhl stood. "Check in regularly and don't hesitate to request backup."

Shane followed him to the door. "I'll call in every three to four hours." Unless he was being shot at. But he knew Ruhl's reminder wasn't about that. When an investigator got deep into a case, sometimes he forgot to check in, leaving himself vulnerable and with no starting place for his backup to pick up his trail in the event of trouble.

Ruhl reached into his jacket pocket and withdrew a set of keys. "Martinez said not to get a scratch on his new car."

Ric Martinez was another Colby Agency alumni and Shane would have much preferred a rental to Martinez's new Mustang.

"A rental might have been a better idea," Shane

suggested even as he took the keys to the hot rod Martinez's wife had bought him for his birthday.

Ruhl laughed. "I think he just wants to prove to you that his Mustang is every bit as cool as your Harley."

"Yeah, right." Something else that wasn't going to happen in this lifetime.

When Ruhl was on his way, Shane put on a fresh pot of coffee and decided to check on Mary Jane. He'd figured Ruhl's visit would rouse her.

She'd left the door to her room open, indicating she'd been pretty shaken up last night. Or maybe she'd been afraid to shut herself off from his line of vision. As he reached the open doorway the first thing that snagged his attention was the waves of silky red hair splayed across the white sheet. His gut clenched and his fingers itched to touch that shiny mane.

Idiot.

Her eyelids fluttered and that wide blue gaze locked on his. The tightness in his chest had to be related to how vulnerable she'd been last night. How easily she could have been hurt…this sweet woman who had never hurt anyone. He'd always had a soft spot for people like her.

But he feared it wasn't as simple as that.

The tightness in other parts of his body warned that his conclusion was far too accurate for his comfort and at the same time completely unrelated to his need to protect.

She pushed the hair out of her face as she sat up, then stretched.

The faded blue shirt he'd given her to sleep in made her deeper blue eyes even more vivid and looked good against her pale skin.

"What time is it?" She picked up her cell from the bedside table. "My phone's dead."

"About eight-thirty." His voice sounded rusty, prompting him to clear his throat. "There's coffee."

She inhaled deeply and smiled. "I smell it." She drew the covers up around her. "I guess I should get dressed."

That was when his heart stumbled. He'd never seen anyone look quite so beautiful as she did at that moment. All rumpled and sexy despite the fact that she was covered completely. It was about the most sensual image he'd ever laid eyes on.

"Nicole—" he looked away "—one of our female investigators—brought over some things from your house that she thought you might need."

"Clothes, I hope."

"Yeah." He swallowed the crazy emotion swelling in his throat. "I'll be right back."

Shane went to get the bag Ruhl had left, cursing himself every step of the way. What the hell was wrong with him? He clenched and unclenched the fingers of his left hand. His arm was as sore as hell. He was sleep deprived. Evidently, his brain had gone into hibernation. He wasn't getting involved with anyone else. One-night stands, occasional dates, that was his social life now. No more relationships. No more commitments.

The truly bizarre part was that this—whatever the hell this was—had happened literally overnight.

"Fool," he muttered as he grabbed the bag.

He'd given himself a good swift mental kick by the time he reached her door once more. And with one look he lost his balance all over again.

She was out of bed, the shirt hanging just past the tops of her thighs, thighs that led to toned calves and on to small, bare feet that were ridiculously distracting.

"Thanks." She grabbed the bag. "I hope my phone charger is in there." The bag plopped onto the bed and she dug through it. "Great." She quickly plugged in her phone, bending and reaching, driving him a little crazier than he clearly already was. "My sister might call again," she said as she faced him once more. "I know it was her voice."

He nodded. "We have someone working on that. If another call comes in they'll conduct a voice analysis to confirm your conclusion."

She chewed her lip a second then asked, "Do I have time to shower?"

"Sure."

Shane pivoted and walked away. This time he didn't stop until he was outside. The idea of her naked…of her smoothing his soap over her skin had him hard all over. He needed some air. The colder the better.

THE COLD HAD CREPT INTO HER bones despite the heavy coat and gloves she wore.

"That's him," Shane said as a man came out of the house they had under surveillance in the Oak Park neighborhood. "Mackey's best friend, Jose Torres."

Mary Jane leaned forward to peer at the man. "I don't remember ever seeing him before." But that didn't mean anything. She'd only seen Jason Mackey once. "Are we going to follow him?"

Shane made no move to start the car. "No. We want to talk to his girlfriend."

"Okay." She wasn't sure what talking to his girlfriend would accomplish, but she wasn't the investigator.

"Teresa Thomas was Jason Mackey's live-in girlfriend right up to the time he started dating Rebecca." Shane looked at Mary Jane then. "She should be willing to give us any dirt she knows on the guy since he dumped her for another woman."

The decision to go for the girlfriend over Torres made sense, considering that information.

Before Shane opened his door to get out of the car, Mary Jane asked, "Is that your ex?" She hadn't meant to ask. It just kind of popped out. But there was a picture of a beautiful woman on the visor and she wondered. If Shane was finished with his ex, why keep a picture of her around where he had to look at it every day?

He glanced at the photo clipped to the driver's-side visor. "That's Piper, the wife of one of my colleagues, Ric Martinez." He cut her a sidelong look. "And the owner of this car."

Oh. "I thought this was your car."

"Afraid not. I'm a Harley man."

She intended to get out of the car before he came around to her door to open it, but she just sat there, remembering the way he'd mounted the bike. The way he'd looked astride it. Even the leather jacket, securely patched on the left sleeve with handy black duct tape, held that air of mystique…of danger.

Yes, he was right. He was a Harley man.

And she was so out of her element here.

No matter, she followed him to the home of Jose Torres. Shane rang the bell and waited. Mary Jane huddled in her coat. It was mercilessly cold this morning. The bitter edge to the climate should have kept her mind off the smell of the soap—his soap— she'd used that morning. But it didn't.

The door opened, and a petite, dark-haired woman looked from Shane to Mary Jane. Her eyes went wide as if she feared Immigration had come to take her boyfriend.

"Teresa Thomas?" Shane displayed his credentials, which looked remarkably like FBI credentials.

The woman swallowed visibly and looked to Mary Jane once more. "Yes?"

"We have some questions to ask you regarding Jason Mackey."

Strangely, her anxiety didn't visibly abate. "He's dead," she said stiffly.

"Yes," Shane said, "that's right. But we have a few questions regarding his activities just prior to his death."

"I spoke to the police and the feds last year," she protested, sounding a bit more confident. "I told them I didn't know anything."

"But you do know something," Shane pressed.

Startled, Mary Jane stared at him. He hadn't said anything about this part to her.

Teresa blinked but didn't deny his assertion.

"He cheated on you to help out a relative and you weren't happy."

As if she'd snapped out of a coma she reached for the door to shut it in his face. Shane flattened his palm against it and held it open.

"You don't have to talk to us," he offered, "but if I push the issue, the feds will be back around to see you."

"If Mitchell comes snooping back around here, I'm filing charges," she threatened, her booming voice overriding her petite size.

Mitchell. Marshal Derrick Mitchell, Shane's former partner. The man who'd stolen his wife.

Mary Jane had a very bad feeling about motive here. Was this about Jason Mackey or Shane Allen?

"Answer our questions," Shane said, "and you won't be hearing from Mitchell."

The exchange went back and forth another minute before Teresa relented and asked them in. "My boyfriend'll be back soon so we gotta make this fast."

Shane fired question one at her before she'd offered them a seat. "What did you know about Mackey's relationship with Rebecca Brooks?"

"I know she was using him," Teresa said with obvious disdain.

"That's impossible," Mary Jane denied. Both Shane and the other woman stared at her. She hadn't meant to say it out loud. But she just couldn't believe her sister would be capable of what Teresa Thomas was suggesting.

"She came after him," Teresa said bitterly. "She took him places he hadn't been before. Spent big money on him. I didn't have a chance against that."

She was wrong. There was no way Rebecca did any such thing, but this time Mary Jane kept her mouth shut. If this woman figured out she was Rebecca's sister she might not tell them whatever Shane seemed to think she knew.

"The cops believe Mackey sought her out. That he killed her."

Teresa shook her head adamantly. "No way.

Jason wasn't a killer. I know what they said," she added vehemently. "Jason couldn't stand his cousin. He wouldn't have worked for him for anything."

"Anthony Chambers," Shane clarified. "You're saying Jason hated Anthony."

"I told the cops that. But they didn't listen. They wanted to blame her disappearance on Jason, and that's what they did."

"Her remains were found in the building where he died," Shane countered.

"Yeah, well, that had to be Anthony's doing. Jason was in love with her. He would have done anything to help her."

"Even hire someone to die in her place?" Shane suggested.

Teresa's eyes rounded, but her expression closed up tightly. "I don't know what you're talking about." She took a step back as if she feared just her proximity would somehow give away something she didn't want to.

"I think you do," Shane pushed. "I think you know exactly what he did."

"You should leave now." She hugged her arms around herself. "Jose will be back and he—"

"Will find out you lied to him," Shane finished for her, "to cover for your ex."

How did he know all this? Was he guessing? Mary Jane was blown away by the turn this interview had taken.

"He can't know." Teresa's voice was shaking now. "He'd kill me." She glanced at Mary Jane. "When me and Jason broke up, I wasn't supposed to talk to him anymore."

"You mean when you started cheating with Jason's best friend."

There was no way Mary Jane could have missed the bitterness in Shane's voice. She wondered if he knew he wasn't over his ex yet.

"It wasn't like that," she practically wailed. "Jason was too busy with Rebecca Brooks to care what I was doing."

"But they had a business deal, not a relationship," Shane said.

"That's the way it started but he told me—" she poked her chest with her thumb "—that he was in love with her and he was going to get her out of the trouble she was in."

"But Torres was working with Chambers, and Jason needed your help."

Fear skated across her face. "I didn't do anything."

"But you told him when Torres was going to make his move."

Teresa looked from Shane to Mary Jane and back once more. "I didn't want Chambers to make a killer out of Jose. He wasn't that kind of man."

"So, Chambers ordered Torres to kill her and Jason got in the way."

She shook her head. "I don't know what happened.

All I know was Rebecca Brooks disappeared and Jason was dead. Jose swears he didn't have anything to do with it."

"But you didn't tell this to the police."

Another frantic shake of her head. "I couldn't. I was afraid. Jose said we'd both end up dead if I said a word. And he swore he didn't kill either one of them." She held Shane's gaze for an extended moment. "I believed him then. I still believe him. He wouldn't lie to me like that."

Shane took a card from his pocket and handed it to her. "Call me if you think of anything useful. Keep in mind that if Torres knows anything, sooner or later he'll end up dead. Chambers isn't going to allow any loose ends."

Mary Jane was pretty sure she would never forget the sheer terror in the other woman's eyes. She had about a dozen questions for Shane, but kept quiet until they were in the car and leaving the neighborhood behind.

"How did you know all that?"

He glanced at her, his expression grim. "Most of it was guesswork."

He put in a call to Simon Ruhl and asked for surveillance on Jose Torres and his current residence.

When he'd finished the call, Mary Jane started to ask if any of it was based on personal experience, but her cell phone rang.

Unknown caller.

Her pulse reacted to an adrenaline rush.

"This might be her," she said, her voice trembling.

He looked from the phone to her. "Answer it."

Mary Jane pressed the necessary button. "Hello?"

"MJ?"

Rebecca.

Mary Jane's heart slammed against her rib cage. "Rebecca, where are you?"

The voice that was surely her sister's whispered an address then urged, "Hurry!"

The dead air told Mary Jane the call had ended.

She stared at the phone. This was the second call. That had to mean her sister was alive. No one could fake two calls...could they?

"What did she say?" Shane prompted, his voice firm.

Her gaze connected with his. Mary Jane repeated the address, a kind of numbness overtaking her, making her tone flat and emotionless. She shifted her attention to the street as her thoughts flew in a thousand directions. "She said to hurry."

Chapter Ten

The street Rebecca had named was part of a neigh-borhood on the verge of extinction—the dilapidated homes were way overdue for demolition. This wasn't exactly a safe place to be even during the daylight hours. Certainly not the sort of place he would expect Mary Jane's sister to hang out.

Shane didn't like this, he didn't like it one little bit. He'd put in a call to Simon Ruhl to let him know their destination and reason for going. Whether or not backup would be needed was yet to be seen. If Rebecca Brooks was here they didn't want to risk spooking her. But he didn't expect that to be the case.

Mary Jane turned all the way around in her seat and surveyed the sad structures they passed. "Does anyone live here?"

"Not legally." He slowed as they neared the block designated by the call. "Homeless folks have taken over the slightly more livable properties, but even those aren't safe. No running water or electricity. Roofs falling in. Not exactly decent living conditions."

"Why doesn't the city tear all this down?"

"Eventually they will. This section of town isn't exactly a high priority on anyone's list."

She collapsed back against the seat. "I don't understand why she would ask us to come here. It doesn't make sense."

Before he could answer, she asked, "Do you think she's been hiding someplace like this so no one could find her?"

He considered the question a moment. Any response was assuming Rebecca Brooks was actually still alive, and that had not been confirmed as of yet. "If your sister is still alive, I'm certain she would want to hide in the last place anyone who knew her would look."

Shane parked the Mustang three houses away from their destination. The street appeared deserted but that didn't mean there wasn't trouble lurking nearby. He didn't like this situation. Walking into these circumstances with a civilian was plain dumb. But he hadn't been able to talk her out of coming.

As naïve as she might be, she was damned determined.

"This is one of those moments," he turned to face her, "where you need to listen carefully to my instructions and do exactly as I tell you."

She nodded slowly. "Okay."

He surveyed the abandoned relics on either side of the street. "I don't like this. Trouble could be hiding anywhere."

"But you said you didn't think those men were trying to kill anyone last night."

His gaze connected with hers. "That's right. I don't. But that doesn't mean that for whatever reasons that we aren't targets today. We don't know the end game, Mary Jane. We don't know the players, the goal, nothing. We can only speculate, assimilate profiles. This—" he looked around again "—is real time. Not strategy, not profiling. If we get out of this car, we're open targets with nothing between us and the enemy. If we walk into that house we could be walking into a trap that we won't be walking out of."

She stared at the house three doors down and heaved a ragged breath. "Well, we'll never know as long as we keep sitting here."

Determined and brave. He resisted the urge to shake his head.

"All right. Stay behind me at all times. Do what I say when I say it. No questions, no hesitation." He searched her eyes as she nodded her agreement. "Let's do it."

They climbed out of the car simultaneously. He met her at the front bumper. "Remember, stay behind me."

He continually surveyed the area, left to right and

back, as they covered the thirty yards to their destination. The porch looked ready to collapse.

"Careful," he warned, as he crossed the creaking boards. "And remember, no sudden moves unless I tell you otherwise."

The interior of the house was dimly lit. Most of the windows were broken and boarded up. The smell of rotting carpet and mold met him at the door. He withdrew his Glock and braced for trouble.

Mary Jane stayed closed behind him. He slowed his respiration and focused on listening and watching for any sound…any movement.

The front room was clear. He moved into the kitchen area. More of that rotting stench.

His gaze landed on a body stretched facedown on the ragged linoleum and he stopped. "Don't move," he warned her as he moved closer to the body. The victim clutched a nine millimeter in his right hand.

Her gasp told him she'd spotted the body.

"Stay put," he reminded as he crouched down next to the vic. Male. Dressed in business attire. Judging by the amount of blood beneath the body this guy was a goner. A check of the carotid artery confirmed his estimation. "Call 9-1-1."

As she made the call, Shane reached into the man's hip pocket for his wallet. Since his face was down against the floor, Shane couldn't ID him without moving the body, and he didn't want to do that.

A gold homicide shield glinted when he opened the wallet.

Detective Brandon Bailen.

"It's Bailen." He looked up at Mary Jane. "He's dead."

"Put your hands up, Allen!"

The order came from behind Mary Jane. She whirled around and Shane flinched. *No sudden moves, damn it.*

"Marshal Mitchell?"

"Step aside, Ms. Brooks," Mitchell ordered. "No one has to get hurt."

Shane eased to his feet, careful to keep the move slow and even. "What's going on, Mitchell?"

"Lay the weapon on the ground," Mitchell told him as he moved fully into the room. Mary Jane had backed out of his way. "Then slide it toward me."

"We just got here, Mitchell. And this is the way we found him."

"That's right," Mary Jane urged. "He was lying there just like that when we walked in."

"I suppose coming here was another of your anonymous tips," Mitchell smirked.

"Don't push me, Mitchell," Shane warned. "I'm not taking this crap from you. My weapon—" he showed the man his Glock "—hasn't even been fired."

"Maybe not," Mitchell countered, "but I'll bet the thirty-eight I found in the yard has been."

What the hell was he talking about? "What thirty-eight?" He hadn't seen any weapon on the ground. But then he hadn't actually been looking for one.

"I said put the Glock down," Mitchell snapped.

The way his face was contorted with frustration or anger, Shane figured he'd be better off playing along. Mary Jane had already called for help. The only thing they could do at this point was play this out and hope the response time in this neighborhood was decent.

Shane dropped into a crouch without taking his eyes off Mitchell and the forty-caliber aimed directly at him. He placed his Glock on the floor and stood, then toed it across the scarred linoleum. "There you go. Happy now?"

"I don't know what's going on here, Allen, but you've got yourself in a hell of a tight spot."

"This is crazy," Mary Jane fairly shouted. "We just got here. Aren't you listening? He was dead already."

Mitchell divided his attention between Shane and Mary Jane. "I received a tip, too," he said to Shane. "And it included a man matching your description and a gun tossed to the ground at the side of the house."

"You really think this is going to be that easy?" Shane laughed. "Someone is setting us up. Maybe that someone is you or maybe you're supposed to take the fall with me. Whatever the case, we're being played. This is going to get ugly fast. A dead cop and two feuding U.S. marshals. Not good."

"You're not a marshal anymore," Mitchell

snarled. "They're sure as hell not going to take your word over mine."

"What about mine?" Mary Jane demanded as she took a step in his direction.

Mitchell's attention whipped toward her and Shane's chest morphed into a vise, squeezing all the air out of his lungs. "Let's just stay cool. We both know neither of us did this," Shane urged. "We can't let the past distort the present. That won't do anyone any good."

If Mitchell was dirty, this situation could deteriorate fast. As much as Shane despised the man, he couldn't say he'd ever had reason to consider him dirty on that level.

The distant wail of sirens had Mitchell lowering his weapon. "We'll have some answers now."

The next few minutes were a blur of activity. What appeared to be half of Chicago PD's force descended upon the neighborhood. Victoria Colby-Camp, Ian Michaels and Simon Ruhl arrived, as did FBI Agent LeMire and his partner. The only person missing was Rebecca Brooks.

If she was alive, what the hell kind of game was she playing?

"VICTORIA, YOUR PEOPLE CAN GO," Police Chief Lawrence Wynne announced, nearly two hours after Shane's arrival on the scene. "As you know, there may be need for additional interviews."

"Of course," Victoria allowed. "Thank you, Chief."

Shane ushered Mary Jane along behind Victoria and the others from the Colby Agency. More than two dozen of Chicago's finest were combing the area for witnesses and/or evidence.

Marshals Mitchell and Bolton stood near Mitchell's car. The exchange looked anything but cordial. Whatever was going on, it wasn't going to help the feds with their case against Horizon Software. Shane didn't feel the least bit sorry for his ex-partner. The guy deserved to be taken down a notch or two.

Condescending jerk.

"We didn't have any luck with the trace on the last call you received from your sister," Ian informed Mary Jane as they reached the Mustang.

"But the recording is in voice analysis as we speak," Victoria added. "We'll soon know if this caller is your sister or someone using previous recordings of her voice to manufacture the necessary dialogue for these calls."

Mary Jane shrugged. "It's her voice. I know her voice." She chewed her lower lip as was her habit when she was confused or worried. "Except when she gave me the house number and street…that part sounded…strange."

"We'll know soon," Ian assured her.

"Research is narrowing down the list of ortho-dontists in St. Louis," Victoria noted, bringing them up to speed on that aspect of the investigation. "We should know something soon on that."

"Meanwhile," Shane put in, "we're going back to pay Jose Torres a visit. According to his girlfriend, Jason Mackey's former lover, Torres knew a hit had been put out on Rebecca, but he didn't get the call to do the job."

"No need," Ian informed him. "Right before we received the call to come here, surveillance discovered the vehicle belonging to Jose Torres in the parking lot of an abandoned gas station. He'd apparently committed suicide."

Shane glanced in the direction of Mitchell and the other feds. "Looks like everyone involved in the case against Horizon Software is on a very short list." His gaze settled on Victoria's. "And it's getting shorter all the time."

MARY JANE SAT VERY STILL in the passenger seat of the Mustang as they drove away from the house where Detective Bailen had been murdered.

Had it just been yesterday that he had come to her door to tell her about the remains linked to Rebecca? How could this be happening?

She had never seen a murdered person before. It was very different from watching her mother take her last breath…or finding her father in his bed after dying in his sleep.

Her entire being shuddered.

"Stop the car!"

Shane only hesitated a moment then he wheeled over to the curb. She jerked free of her safety belt and flung the door open. No sooner than her feet hit the grass beyond the cracked sidewalk then her stomach heaved. Her entire body started to shake, and it was all she could do to remain partially vertical.

Since she'd forgone breakfast that morning, there wasn't much to lose, but lose it she did.

When her stomach had stopped its involuntary spasms, she became aware of Shane standing a couple of steps behind her.

"I found this in the glove box." He passed her a couple of fast-food napkins and a piece of peppermint candy wrapped in the logo of a popular drive-through.

"Thanks." She wiped her lips and took a couple of deep breaths before she dared to pop the mint into her mouth. She was thankful for the pleasant flavor to chase away the bitter aftertaste.

Shane waited patiently; didn't rush her to get back into the car. When she felt steady enough she climbed back into the fancy car and thanked God she hadn't puked on the floorboard. She doubted Shane's colleague would have appreciated that.

"Could you handle some ginger ale or a soft drink?" He started the engine, checked his mirrors and eased back onto the street.

"I'd like to go home." She needed to change

clothes. Brush her teeth. And just lie down in her own bed and think. She'd hardly slept at all last night. She kept thinking about the man across the hall and all this insanity. Unfortunately, one had had nothing to do with the other. Her crazy thoughts about Shane had been purely the selfish physical kind.

She shook off the memories and focused her bleary mind on the here and now.

Was he right about the people involved in the case against Horizon Software? Were they being murdered one by one? Was she on that list?

And where was her sister?

Mary Jane closed her eyes and let her head drop back against the headrest. There were no answers. Only questions.

"I'll take you home for a little while."

"Then what?" she asked weakly. She sounded like death warmed over. Sick and frail. And all this time she'd thought she was so strong. *Ha!* She wasn't strong, she was a coward. The entire time her mother had been ill, Rebecca had insisted that she could recover all the way up to the day she died. That there was hope. Not Mary Jane. As soon as the doctor had said their mother was dying, she had accepted that fate and then went about seeing after her mother until the end. Not once had she believed a miracle could happen.

She wasn't strong enough to believe in miracles.

Maybe her sister was alive. She certainly was

strong enough to take control of her life and try and prevent the inevitable.

Did that make her a bad person? A deserter?

Mary Jane just didn't know.

"After that," Shane said in answer to her question, "we'll see if we can get anywhere near Torres's girlfriend again."

"You think she knows more than she's telling?" She had seemed pretty terrified of ratting on her boyfriend.

"Maybe, maybe not. But with Torres dead, there's always the chance her story may have changed dramatically."

Before Mary Jane could ask anything else, Shane's cell phone rang.

"Allen."

She waited while he listened to the caller.

"We're on our way."

When he'd put the phone away, she asked, "More surprises?"

He looked directly into her eyes for as long as he dared and still navigate the traffic. "Ann Martin, one of my colleagues, has been watching your apartment."

She hoped her place hadn't burned down or exploded. She'd definitely watched too many plot-challenged action movies.

"You received a FedEx package."

Confusion worried her brow, adding to the

ache gathering there. She didn't remember ordering anything. She supposed it could be some gift from a relative who wanted to show sympathy for the loss of her parents. A card still trickled in now and again.

"The package," he went on, "is from your sister."

"Oh, my God." Mary Jane's stomach clenched. "Does this mean she's really alive?"

He didn't answer immediately. His fingers were clenched tightly around the steering wheel and he kept his focus on the street. The grim set of his jaw gave nothing away. She hadn't noticed until then that he hadn't shaved that morning. The stubble that darkened his jaw made him look all the more dangerous. The goatee and longish hair and leather made her think again of a pirate.

Okay, her mind was rambling now. She had to focus.

"Shane?" It was the first time she'd called him by his first name. She wasn't sure how she felt about that. At some point, she'd decided to *think* of him as Shane.

He braked for the traffic light as it turned red. When he'd come to a complete stop, he turned to look directly at her. "It was overnighted yesterday afternoon from a downtown service center. According to Martin, the package was mailed by a female. The clerk couldn't remember what she looked like. Dark sunglasses and a scarf that covered her hair."

Mary Jane gripped the armrest more tightly as if

that might steady the way her mind was whirling. If Rebecca was alive and putting her through this hell, Mary Jane was going to be seriously ticked off.

Her sister would have some powerful explaining to do if she really had been alive all this time.

And if she wasn't…

Then Mary Jane would…be all alone just like she had been since she'd buried their father.

"Did she…" Mary Jane cleared the emotion from her throat. "Did your colleague open the package?"

"Yes."

She took a breath, let it out. "So are you going to tell me what was in it or do I have to guess?"

"There's a key."

"A key?" First there was the condo and the vehicle. What now? "What kind of key?"

"Martin thinks it's to a safety deposit box. They're trying to run down the possibilities."

She didn't remember ever hearing Rebecca talk about a safety deposit box, and Mary Jane sure didn't have one.

"Is that all?" Surely there was more than just that.

"There was a note."

Frustration rifled through her. "Would you just tell me already?"

He still didn't make eye contact. "We'll be there soon. We'll have all the facts then."

There was something bad he wasn't telling her.

Her stomach churned violently.

Maybe he was afraid she'd mess up his friend's car. Or maybe he just didn't want to deal with her hysteria. And right now it was rising fast. Really fast.

Chapter Eleven

The key.

Mary Jane sat in the middle of her living room floor and stared at the key in her palm.

Ann Martin, Shane's colleague from the Colby Agency, had determined that the key definitely came from a bank. But which one wasn't known yet.

Grasping the key in her right hand, she reached for the card with her left. She reread the single line for the third or fourth time. She couldn't remember, she'd lost count. Maybe she'd read it a dozen times already.

You know the place.

"Bec, why did you do this?"

Simon Ruhl had gone to the FedEx service center with a picture of Rebecca, and the clerk still couldn't identify her as the woman who had mailed the package. But she couldn't say it wasn't her, either.

Everything was going further and further out of control. The thirty-eight suspected of being used to kill

Detective Bailen had been wiped clean of prints. Jose Torres's girlfriend had vanished. And there hadn't been any more calls to Mary Jane's cell. The voice analysis on the one recorded wasn't complete yet.

They knew nothing, and two people were dead.

Besides Rebecca.

If Rebecca was dead.

Shane settled on the floor next to her, his arms propped on his knees. "We'll figure it out eventually. Don't beat yourself up if nothing comes to mind. We all remember things differently. What may have been a particularly vivid memory to your sister may have barely registered for you."

Mary Jane drew her knees up to her chest and wrapped her arms around them. "She must have believed I would remember. She had it right with the Monopoly property card." Opening her hand, she stared at the key again. "I don't think she would get this wrong. Not if it's important, and it must be important."

"Close your eyes."

Resting her cheek against her knees, she studied his intent expression. He had the most intense eyes she had ever seen. "That's not going to help."

"Maybe not." The ghost of a smile lingered on his lips. "Doesn't hurt to try."

"Fine." She closed her eyes. "Now what?"

"Think back as far as you can. To your earliest memories with your sister."

That was easy. She and Bec had been five and seven. Their first trip to Disney World. Their parents had been young and healthy. Life had been good.

Her breath caught at the feel of a warm fingertip pushing the hair back from her face. Heat flared inside her and her lids fluttered open. He was watching her with those dark eyes.

"You were smiling. I think that's the first time I've seen you smile like that. Like you mean it."

She lifted her head and sighed. "I have a lot of good memories of my family, but I'm not sure this is going to work."

"If you were kids, the bank would likely have been one your parents used. Probably here in the city."

Her parents had always used First Federal Bank as far back as she could remember. That was the one they had used until the very end.

"Did you check First Federal already?"

He nodded.

Made sense. She'd already told him that was the one her parents had used.

"You don't think it was a bank in St. Louis, do you?" If that were the case, she might never figure this out. She'd been thirteen when they'd moved to Chicago. There were a million things about life in St. Louis that she had forgotten.

"No problem." He pushed to his feet and offered his hand. "Maybe what you need is a visual aid."

"What?" Even as she asked for clarification, she placed her hand in his.

"If Rebecca expected you to remember it, then the place must have had a visual impact on the two of you. Come on."

He led the way to her home office, where his associate worked on a laptop she'd brought with her.

"Ann, could we have a copy of that list?" He flashed Mary Jane a smile. "We're going to take a little road trip."

Ann passed him the requested list. Blond hair and green eyes, Ann Martin looked to be about twenty-five, but considering her banking background she had to be at least thirty. She was tall and thin like a runway model.

"I'll let you know if I have any hits here."

Shane gave her a little salute and then gestured for Mary Jane to precede him. They grabbed their coats on the way through her living room. She'd changed into jeans and a sweater as soon as they'd arrived at her apartment. Washed her face and brushed her teeth twice.

Hopefully, she could get through whatever came next without another distasteful incident.

He opened the Mustang's passenger door and waited for her to settle inside. Then he rounded the hood and slid behind the wheel. He passed the list to her.

"Where to first?"

As he cranked the engine she surveyed the names of financial institutions. Might as well start at the top.

"The Mag Mile."

THE FIRST HALF-DOZEN BANKS didn't stir the slightest memory. She'd known just driving past that she hadn't been there before.

By the time they'd hit the double digits, Mary Jane was beginning to think maybe her sister really had selected a bank from their old hometown, St. Louis.

And then a memory clicked.

The First Savings and Trust.

Bold, Grecian architecture. Magnificent. Grand. A palace fit for a princess.

"This is it." Her heart smashed against her rib cage.

Shane drove past the institution to find a parking spot. When he'd eased the Mustang between two other vehicles, she was out before he'd shut off the engine. Anticipation seared through her veins.

"We came here when I was nine. We were visiting my grandparents," she told him as he joined her on the sidewalk. "They used this bank." She surveyed the massive structure. Beautiful. "I told my sister that when I grew up I was going to marry a prince and live in a house just like this."

"You had good taste for a nine-year-old."

Mary Jane reached into her coat pocket and retrieved the key. "Let's see if this is the place."

They walked up the steps to the main entrance.

He kept his hand against her back. She liked that he made that connection, protective and caring. Kept the "alone" feelings at bay.

Inside, their shoes clicked on the marble floor. The towering ceiling made her think of an eloquent museum. The architecture was amazing. Ornate and timeless as if it had been transported from a centuries-old European city.

Shane was right. She'd definitely had good taste as a kid. Too bad the dream hadn't worked out. She glanced at the man next to her. Or had it?

At one of the customer service desks, Shane smiled for the tellee and she was instantly charmed. "We need to access a safety deposit box."

"Right this way."

As the woman led the way to another desk, Mary Jane whispered, "What if this isn't the right bank?"

"Then we'll know in a minute," he whispered back.

That was true.

"Mr. Trenton will take care of you," the tellee said with a smile.

Shane thanked her.

"Sign in here, please," Mr. Trenton instructed.

Mary Jane, her heart thudding, sat down at the desk and picked up a pen to sign the register, which reminded her of an old-fashioned hotel registry.

She held her breath as he read her name, then typed the information into his computer.

"May I see some ID, Ms. Brooks?"

Did that mean her name was in there? Surely, if it wasn't he would have just said so.

Her fingers trembling, she reached into her purse and fished out her wallet. She provided her driver's license and waited, hoping against hope this was the place.

"Very well." Mr. Trenton passed the license back to her.

She took it, her heart at a near standstill waiting for him to tell her something one way or another.

"You have your key, I presume."

She nodded and showed him the key.

"This way." He stood. "Is the gentleman going to accompany you?"

"Yes…if that's all right."

"Just sign in, sir, and show me your ID."

Shane did as instructed, and then they followed Mr. Trenton into the bank's massive vault room, which contained hundreds upon hundreds of secured boxes.

Mr. Trenton walked straight over to the rear wall and inserted his key into box 414. Mary Jane was overjoyed that she hadn't had to ask him the box number. She was pretty sure he would have seen that as suspicious behavior. Her head was reeling with the idea that her signature had somehow been on file. Had Rebecca forged her name? Her hand still shaking, she thrust her key into the second lock and gave it a turn. Evidently so.

Trenton removed the box and carried it to a nearby table. Each table had privacy sides that prevented anyone except the person at that particular section from seeing the contents of the box. Each section contained a brass desk lamp and a desktop computer.

Mr. Trenton gifted her with a polite smile. "Take your time."

Mary Jane sat down at the table, mainly because her legs had gone unsteady beneath her. Shane stood next to her.

"Would you like me to open it?"

She sucked in a harsh breath. "No. I've got it."

The box wasn't one of the large ones. Regular size. Gray metal. Nothing special. And yet her sister had left her a message here.

"Okay." She lifted the lid and stared at the contents. One CD and one white business-size envelope with her name written on it.

Mary Jane picked up the envelope and opened the unsealed flap. A single piece of paper was folded in the same manner as a typical business letter. Emotion filled her eyes as she visually identified the handwriting as her sister's.

Dear Mary Jane,

I am so sorry for any pain this situation may have caused you. I left you the videotaped message at the condo in hopes that if anyone were watching you that they would assume you knew nothing and would stop. The little game using the Monopoly card was to give the plan credibility. I pray it worked.

The idea of my former employer getting away with what he did prompted me to make other arrangements for covering that possibility. The FedEx package was to be delivered in the event I died. So, if you've come here, then there is reason to believe I am dead. The woman I paid to deliver the package has heard news that this is the case and has set this phase of my plan in motion. The CD contains copies of everything the FBI will need to take Anthony Chambers down. I have provided this same evidence already but, if I'm dead, I suspect it was covered up.

Therein lies my one problem. Someone working my case is dirty. I don't know who. We tried to figure it out, but couldn't. So be very, very careful who you give this to. Otherwise, it will all be for nothing.

Jason is trying to help me escape the inevitable. He loves me, MJ. He would do anything for me. If he is still alive when this is over, thank him. He tried hard to help.

Do what you have to do, but be careful.

I love you,

Bec

Somehow Mary Jane managed not to cry. Maybe it was because of the strength she had felt as she'd read her sister's letter. She should have known better than to doubt Rebecca. No way would she have been involved in anything wrong.

"We can't walk out of here with that," Shane said quietly. "If we do, it'll be like stamping a huge bull's-eye on our foreheads."

"Will it be okay to leave it here?" She'd never had a safety deposit box before. Seemed safe enough, but then, what did she know?

"The bank's not going to let anyone near it without a court order, and if we're dealing with a dirty fed the last thing he's going to want to do is leave a paper trail." Shane seemed to consider their options a moment. "But before we go, I'd like to know what's on that CD." He gestured to the computer. "Let's have a look."

Mary Jane removed the CD from its protective holder and placed it into the appropriate slot. A few seconds later she opened a document that listed dates, locations and transactions. She and Shane studied the information as they moved from document to document. Digital shots of faxes and e-mails. Unbelievable. Anthony Chambers had been selling secrets to terrorists! Middle Eastern, Russian, you name it. This looked to be sufficient evidence to nail him to the wall, in Mary Jane's opinion.

"Before we put that away—" Shane crouched down next to her "—I'm going to take some snapshots of key pieces of evidence with the camera in my phone and send it to the Colby Agency for safekeeping." His gaze fixed on hers. "Just in case."

"Sounds like a smart move."

She watched as he made snapshot after snapshot, checking each one to make sure it was readable. Then he forwarded each one to his associate, Simon Ruhl. When he'd finished, Mary Jane placed the CD back into its case and returned both it and the letter to the safety deposit box. Shane carried the box back to its slot in the wall of boxes and slid it into place. Mr. Trenton returned to secure it.

"Do you think they're watching us?" she asked as they strolled out of the vault.

"Yes."

She shuddered at the danger they were both in. And yet, somehow, she felt safe next to this man.

Mary Jane thanked Mr. Trenton on her way out. She glanced back one last time before exiting the main entrance. Her sister had been right to pick this place. There were hardly any grand places like this left anymore. And who knew. Maybe one day she *would* live in a house like this.

But she wouldn't hold her breath.

Like Shane, she exited onto the street with extreme vigilance. The enemy could be anywhere.

Watching. Ready to take action. She wouldn't be forgetting the shoot-out in the middle of the night last night. Or finding Detective Bailen's body today.

They'd gotten settled in the car and Shane had started the engine when his cell rang.

The conversation was pretty much one-sided, but his occasional mono-syllabic response was loaded with disdain.

Had to be Mitchell. His ex-partner was the only person she'd heard him to speak to with such low regard.

When he closed the phone he said, "We have a command performance at the Bureau. LeMire insists on seeing all parties involved. Mitchell and Bolton are on their way there now."

Mary Jane heard what he said, but mostly she was obsessing on the idea that what she'd seen and read in the safety deposit box pretty much confirmed that her sister was dead.

The phone calls had to be fabricated.

A new wave of sadness washed over her. She hadn't really expected Rebecca to still be alive, but it had been kind of nice to believe for just a little while that it might be possible.

She didn't talk as they drove to the FBI headquarters. Shane knew the letter had gotten to her. He wished he could say something to make her feel better, but there was nothing. She would have to grieve the loss of her sister.

Mary Jane had lost every member of her family in the past year.

That had to be tough.

Really tough.

Though he didn't see his family often, they were there. He could visit anytime.

He stopped at the guard shack and showed his ID. When the guard waved him through, he drove onto the lot and parked, then turned to his passenger.

"You okay?"

She shrugged. "I think so. It's just been a lot to deal with."

That was definitely true.

"Let's get this out of the way and we'll find a nice quiet place to eat. I don't know about you, but I'm starved."

"That would be nice."

Halfway across the parking lot, his phone rang again. He paused to take the call. "Allen."

"Shane, this is Simon."

From the sound of his colleague's somber voice, this wasn't going to be good news.

"What's up?" He glanced at Mary Jane, hoping he didn't have to dump anything else on her today.

"We found the orthodontist Rebecca Brooks used. Dr. Leonard Strickland. Fortunately, he still had her file in his office. The M.E.'s office e-mailed a copy of the victim's dental views to Strickland. The victim was positively *not* Rebecca Brooks. We don't have confirmation that the vic was Amanda Ferguson, but it definitely was not Rebecca."

"Thanks. Maybe that's why we were called to the Bureau for a face-to-face."

"I'm not sure they have this information yet. I can be there in fifteen minutes," Ruhl offered.

Shane didn't see any reason for Ruhl to rush over here. "I'll let you know if we need any assistance."

"Also, we expect to have that voice analysis no later than tomorrow morning."

"That'll help." Shane ended the call and dropped the phone back into his pocket.

Mary Jane didn't ask any questions as they continued on toward the lobby of the building, but he knew she needed to know this.

"That was Simon Ruhl. They found the orthodontist in St. Louis. The remains did not belong to Rebecca."

Mary Jane's continued silence told him that she didn't know how to feel. Was Rebecca dead or alive? Either way, where the hell was she?

He could certainly understand that.

Once they were cleared through security, they made the trip to the fourth floor conference room in more of that thickening silence.

Mitchell, Bolton, LeMire and his partner were all on hand. It surprised him that there was no representative from Chicago PD. This was their case, as well. With Bailen dead, evidently the Bureau had opted to leave the whole division out of the loop.

"We have evidence that Detective Brandon Bailen may have been involved in the disappearance of Rebecca Brooks," LeMire announced.

If he'd said Bailen had been resurrected in the morgue, Shane wouldn't have been more surprised.

Before he could say as much, Mary Jane shot out of her chair. "You have to be joking! Detective Bailen was one of the finest policemen I've ever met. He worked hard to solve Rebecca's case. More so than any of you," she stated with a solemn appraisal of those gathered. "I can tell you that."

Shane put his hand on hers and urged her with his eyes to have a seat. No need to let this get out of control right out of the chute.

LeMire spread an array of photos across the table. All showed Rebecca and Bailen in a variety of settings and obviously deep in conversation. One included Jason Mackey, as well.

"That 'for sale' list you discovered with Amanda Ferguson's name on it," LeMire said, "was a case Bailen had pushed aside as unsolvable more than a year ago. Suddenly, the remains for a name on that list shows up in his highest-profile case. Strikes me as a little too coincidental, wouldn't you say?"

Mitchell nodded his agreement. "Other than the four of us—" he indicated the federal agents at the table "—no one else knew the specifics of this case except Bailen."

"So you believe," Shane began, "that Bailen was working with Anthony Chambers."

"It's a significant possibility," Bolton offered. "We have to consider every avenue. He did have one-on-one contact with the key witness in the case." He tapped one of the photos. "Repeatedly."

"I've heard enough." Mary Jane stood once more. "I'm not listening to any more of this. If I were you—" she looked from one man to the other "—I would take a closer look at your own agencies."

She walked out.

Shane had no choice but to follow.

He caught up with her at the elevator.

"They're grasping at straws," he offered, though not really in defense of the men they had left in that conference room but in defense of the agencies they represented.

"Rebecca said—"

He pressed a finger to her lips to quiet her before she said anything about the safety deposit box out loud.

"Not here."

She put her hand to her mouth and turned away from him.

He had to rub his fingers together to erase the feel of her lips. Damn, he had to pull himself together here. This growing obsession he had with the woman was nothing but asking for trouble.

It wasn't until they had cleared the building's front entrance that he felt comfortable talking freely.

"Rebecca could have been right about her suspicions, but we have no proof," he offered quietly to set the tone of the conversation. It wasn't impossible that someone could be listening. No need to take the risk. "We have to see this thing through and get our ducks in a row before we go there."

Mary Jane nodded her understanding. "Someone's using Detective Bailen as a scapegoat."

He had arrived at the same conclusion, but no amount of deductions would do anyone any good without evidence. Shane opened her door and then went around to the driver's side and got behind the wheel.

"Do you think we can do this?"

He slid the key into the ignition as he met her gaze. "Prove one of those guys back there is dirty?"

"Yes."

The uncertainty in those big blue eyes tugged at his heart. He didn't know what the hell he was doing letting this thing between them get out of hand, but he was helpless to stop it.

He shot her a smile, anything to give her the reassurance she needed right now. "Absolutely. Whoever is behind this is already running scared. All we have to do is be there when they screw up."

Her answering smile melted something deep inside him. He was reasonably sure it was his resolve not to feel exactly what he was feeling.

He twisted the car key.

The ignition hesitated.

Adrenaline blasted through his veins.

"Get out of the car!"

Even as he said the words, he reached across her and shoved open her door.

"Get out!" he repeated as he flung open his own door and dove for the pavement.

He hit the asphalt hard then rolled as far and as fast as he could.

An explosion shook the ground.

Parts of the shiny red Mustang flew through the air and showered down upon him.

Mary Jane.

The debris was still flying as he half scrambled, half ran on all fours around to her side of the car.

She lay on the ground…unmoving.

Chapter Twelve

She could see his mouth moving, but the words were so far away she couldn't hear.

Shane.

The ground.

She was lying on the cold asphalt.

Mary Jane tried to sit up but he stopped her.

"Don't move."

She read his lips this time. Why did he sound so far away?

There was a cut on his jaw. Blood dripped like crimson tears.

What happened?

His right hand pressed against her right side. She tried to move away from the pressure but pain arced through her and he pressed even harder so she kept still.

Don't move. Don't move.

Why did her body hurt so badly?

The car.

She turned her head to where the car sat. The hood was partially open, twisted and scrunched as if it had impacted with a tree. Had they hit something? She didn't remember driving out of the parking lot.

The memory of a horrific blast echoed in her head. *Explosion.*

Her heart thumped against her sternum.

Bomb?

But they were okay…weren't they?

She tried to rise up again, but he stopped her.

"You'll be okay."

This time she could hear the words…barely. His voice sounded calm. But it was the fear in his eyes that sent her pulse skittering.

If he was scared, this had to be bad.

Suddenly there were people everywhere…red and blue lights flashing.

Shane was forced back as men in uniforms dropped to their knees next to her. Paramedics.

She should just tell them that she was fine. She tried to lift herself up into a sitting position, but they forced her back down. She tried to speak, but no one appeared to be listening.

Her blouse was cut away from her torso. She started to protest but then she saw the blood.

Her blood on the gloves of the paramedic.

On the dissected blouse.

She was bleeding.

A lot.

The ground tilted, and she felt bile rise in her throat. Not again. She wasn't going to throw up again. No way.

"Ms. Brooks, are you on any medication?" one of the paramedics asked.

"No." Her voice sounded small, but she could hear herself. She heard the paramedics, too.

"You might feel a stick," one said. "Don't be alarmed. It's just the IV drip."

The two tossed so many questions at her that she could barely keep up. She didn't understand what was going on. Was she hurt that badly? Where was Shane?

"We've got the bleeding under control," the paramedic on her left told her. "Your vitals are stable so we're going to transport you to Mercy General and get you taken care of." His eyes offered a warm reassurance with the confident words.

"Okay." She tried to swallow, didn't have any luck. Where was Shane?

Her questions dissolved like so much sugar in the rain when the paramedics moved her onto a gurney. She bit down hard on her lip to hold back a groan at the pain. A crowd of people had gathered around the damaged car and her. Great. She'd always wanted to be a side show for the morbid curiosity of onlookers. Another jolt of pain and she forgot all about them.

As they loaded her into the ambulance, she saw

Shane. He was arguing with the paramedics. The next time she saw him he was sitting on one side of her with a paramedic.

She decided to try for some answers. "What's the damage?" She looked directly at the paramedic as she asked. Shane would only give her a glossed-over version. He'd tell her she was fine and that would be that.

"Ma'am, you have about a six-inch laceration on your right side. We have the bleeding under control and the wound temporarily closed. We'll do a few X-rays just to be sure there's nothing in there that shouldn't be, then we'll do the permanent closure."

"What's your instinct telling you?" She had a right to know. If she was going to need surgery she might as well be prepared.

"Your vitals are stable. That's a good sign. But when you're in the blast zone of an explosion, it's kind of like getting caught in a hurricane where a flimsy broom straw can be driven into a tree trunk. It's best not to take any chances."

"What about him?" She looked from the paramedic to Shane and back.

The paramedic grinned. "He'll get checked out, too. But he appears to be doing just fine."

"Good." Mary Jane closed her eyes without meeting Shane's gaze. She was pretty sure they had given her something for pain in the IV since she felt a little woozy and the pain was practically gone.

She was really glad she wasn't dead. The arrangements weren't made and there wasn't anyone left to take care of those things.

Who took care of that sort of thing for someone who had no one?

She would have to look into that. Assuming she didn't die before she got the chance.

Was this the way Rebecca had lived those last few weeks?

ANN MARTIN MET SHANE AT THE hospital with a change of clothes for Mary Jane. She'd been stitched up, but the doctor on duty wanted a second set of X-rays just in case. Shane was forced to wait in the corridor while the technician did her work. He didn't like it, but there was only a door between him and Mary Jane, so he was dealing with it.

"You look like hell, Allen." Ann surveyed him from head to toe and back.

"Feel like it, too." Scraped and bruised mostly. The sudden lunge to the ground had his hip acting up, but he'd get over that.

"And if I were you," Ann said with a smirk, "I'd be damned glad that Ric Martinez is out of the country. He's going to want to kick your butt when he sees his Mustang."

Shane took the shopping bag containing the change of clothes from her and flashed a fake smile.

"All I can say to that is, he'd better bring his lunch because it's going to take him all day."

Ann laughed. "Hey, I hear Martinez had a similar incident when he first started working with the agency. Something about Ian Michaels's SUV. I'd much rather have Martinez fired up than Ian any day."

Shane couldn't argue that. No one wanted to be on the bad side of the enigmatic Ian Michaels. Maybe it was the vaguely European accent or the way he could cut a hole through a guy with one look.

"Just so you know," Ann went on, "Victoria has already called her insurance claims adjuster. She'll have Martinez a brand-spanking-new car just like the old one before he even hears the news."

Shane was glad to hear it. Most of the damage to the car was under the hood and to the dash. But it was a total loss, no question.

"Any word yet on how the hell someone got to the car with it parked in the Bureau's lot?" he asked. It took an act of Congress to get on the property.

"Surveillance cameras don't show any activity around the car while it was on federal property. Simon thinks maybe it happened while you were at scene of Bailen's murder. The feds are looking into the possibility of a faulty detonator, which may have caused the delay."

"It was tied in to the switch." Shane had felt the hesitation when he'd tried to start the engine. He'd known instantly what it was. Usually a guy didn't live through that kind of epiphany. He and Mary Jane had been damned lucky.

Ann nodded her agreement to his assessment. "If Simon's correct, then the car should have gone boom when you left that crime scene."

Shane replayed their movements that morning. "Then we were doubly lucky because we stopped by her place to see you right after that."

Ann laughed dryly. "You must have a guardian angel, Allen."

But that was just it. He didn't. Otherwise he wouldn't have gotten himself shot last year. Maybe Mary Jane was the one with the guardian angel.

The door opened and the tech rolled Mary Jane from the X-ray room. She hated the wheelchair, but considering the painkillers it was best she didn't try to walk under her own steam.

She spotted the bag right away. "Thank God." She looked up at Ann. "You're a lifesaver."

"No problem, Ms. Brooks." Ann passed a set of keys to Shane. "It's the gray Lexus. The directions to the safe house have been loaded into the navigation system." Ann hesitated before walking away. "Try not to blow up anything else, Allen."

She laughed as she walked away. Shane shook his head. "She'd never make it as a comedian."

Mary Jane searched his face. "Maybe she's flirting with you."

"Now who's the comedian?" He grabbed the wheelchair handles and ushered the patient in the direction of the exam room they'd left a half hour ago.

"She's gorgeous," Mary Jane said, intent on pursuing the subject.

"She's not my type." The image of Mary Jane wearing his shirt and sleeping in his guestroom, her silky red hair spilled across the linens, instantly filled his head.

"Guys always say that about the girls they like when they're afraid of rejection."

"So now you're a female Dr. Phil." He stopped long enough to lean close to her ear. Two could play this game. "You know, it helps if you're speaking from experience."

She folded her arms over her chest and didn't say another word as he transported her back to the exam room. When the doctor had dismissed her and she'd had a chance to change out of the hospital gown, he escorted her to the Lexus in the same wheelchair. She gave him the silent treatment.

Okay, so maybe he'd gone too far with the "experience" remark.

Once she was settled into the passenger seat, he pulled the safety belt across her lap and snapped it into place. He hesitated before withdrawing from the vehicle, put himself nose to nose with her and looked straight into her eyes. "Sorry about that remark. I was out of line."

She lifted her chin, didn't break eye contact. "I guess I asked for it."

The need to lean closer still, to let his lips brush hers was nearly overpowering. Somehow he managed to pull away. He closed the door and went around to the driver's side and got in.

"Ann mentioned a safe house."

Shane shoved the key into the ignition and, despite knowing it was safe to do so, he had to concentrate for a second before turning the ignition. The vehicle's engine hummed to life and he relaxed.

"Victoria's lake house." He glanced at Mary Jane. "You'll like it."

MARY JANE HAD DOSED OFF by the time they reached their destination. The drive seemed to take forever, and she hadn't been able to keep her eyes open any longer. She jumped when Shane placed his hand on her arm.

"We made it. No flying bullets, no explosions."

She moistened her lips. Her mouth felt dry. The drugs. "That's a relief." She'd had enough excitement the past thirty or so hours to last a lifetime or two.

He hurried around to her side of the car and assisted her efforts to get out. She was sore. Especially the side with the ugly laceration. That was definitely going to leave a mark.

She felt a little stronger now. Walking wasn't so awkward. The painkillers had at first made muscle coordination difficult. She didn't enjoy the feeling, though she did appreciate the pain relief.

They entered the house from the garage. She had no idea how massive the house was until she passed through the kitchen and reached the family room.

"This place is huge." She turned around slowly, really slowly, and tried to take in the elegant details. "Wow. It's amazing."

"It's a great place." He reached for her hand. "Check this out."

He led her to the wall of windows that looked out over the lake. The clouds blocked most of the moon, but the few rays that reached through reflected on the black of the water. It looked so still, so peaceful and mysterious. Just like the man next to her.

"Would you like something to drink?"

She wet her lips again. "Water would be great." She hugged her arms around herself, careful of her side, couldn't seem to get warm enough.

"You want to watch some television, or do you need to call it a night?"

From somewhere deep inside her she summoned a halfhearted smile. "You know I think I need to lie down." She felt extremely tired. She had a million questions, but all of it could wait until morning. She just couldn't take anymore stimuli tonight.

Particularly not the kind that involved looking at him. The scratches and bruises that made him look as if he'd been in a barroom brawl. The new rip and scuff marks in what was obviously his favorite leather jacket.

No, she couldn't trust herself in this man's presence a minute longer than necessary right now. Between the drugs and the emotional wasteland that lay in her chest, she was pretty desperate.

He nodded. "I understand."

Shane guided her through the house, letting her set the pace, which was about half that of a snail's. When they reached the second floor, he allowed her first choice of the rooms. She selected one with a lake view. Then he left to fetch the requested bottle of water.

Mary Jane moved across the room to stand at the floor-to-ceiling wall of windows. She stared at the meager light on the dark water and wondered what her life would be like when this was over. Would she learn that her sister was alive and in hiding? Murdered by someone who had sworn to protect her?

At this rate, would Mary Jane even be alive to learn the truth?

Someone certainly wanted her dead.

But why? Until today she hadn't known a thing about the case against Horizon Software.

Now, she knew too much.

She imagined that was what the enemy had been trying to prevent from the beginning.

"Here you go."

She turned around slowly to face the man who'd returned with a bottle of imported water.

"Is what you sent Mr. Ruhl enough to put Anthony Chambers away even if his people succeed in killing us?" She hated that her lips quivered as she asked the question. She'd meant to be strong, to maintain her calm. But she'd failed. The trembling spread, making her feel unsteady.

Shane set the bottle on a table and walked toward her, one deliberate step at a time. "First," he said with quiet determination, "no one's getting to you without going through me. No one could have foreseen what happened today, but we've had fair warning now. That's why we're here where no one can reach us. State-of-the-art security. Unbreachable."

Another step disappeared between them. "Second," he continued with the same confidence, "Simon Ruhl, Ann Martin and Ian Michaels will be handling the investigation from here. My only objective will be to protect you."

Another step. Her breath caught softly.

He stood toe-to-toe with her now. "And no one's getting past me as long as I'm still breathing."

Warmth flowed along her limbs, chasing away the chill she'd felt to some degree since Detective Bailen had shown up at her door. She felt warm and safe. As crazy as it sounded under the circumstances, she was certain this man would do exactly as he said he would, although she'd known him for a time best measured in hours rather than days.

"There's just one other thing," she whispered, her throat aching with the possibility.

"Name it."

She threw caution to the wind, and let herself get completely lost in his dark eyes. That now familiar intensity made her want so desperately to feel it in every imaginable way…to have him want her the way she wanted him.

"I'm sure this is not part of your job, but I really need you to kiss me right now. I can't remember the last time I was kissed but—"

He brushed his lips across hers. Her breath stalled in her chest.

And then he made the seal complete, covering her mouth fully with his own. His fingers curved around her cheeks, slid into her hair, pulled her mouth more firmly against his. And the day—the bullets, the blood, the murder and the bombing— all disappeared.

She dared to flatten her hands against his chest. The feel of the ridged terrain beneath the cotton shirt had her wishing she could feel the heat of his skin. Her body throbbed with a need she hadn't felt in eons. Or maybe ever.

He pulled away from the kiss and her heart stumbled drunkenly. A smile slid across his kiss-dampened lips.

"We're both pretty beat up. I'm not sure we should let this get too far out of bounds."

"In the last twenty-four hours," she said quickly, impulsively, "I've been shot at, interrogated by the federal authorities and bombed. I think we left any sort of boundaries behind a couple of ER visits ago."

He stroked her cheek with his thumb, the feeling incredibly sweet. "This isn't something you jump right into, Mary Jane. Not…under the circumstances."

Thank you, Rebecca. "I'm not a virgin, if that's what you're worried about." There was that one time when she was nineteen and then again when she was twenty-five. Hardly noteworthy experiences, but if he needed her resumé, she had entries. It wasn't a blank page.

His expression closed and he took a step back, physically and emotionally. "This would be a mistake." He gave his head a succinct shake. "I don't do adrenaline-crash sex. You're in no condition to make this kind of decision."

He'd left the room before the shock faded enough for her to summon a response, and then it was too late.

She'd felt and tasted his desire. Was he really that noble, or was this about his ex-wife?

Maybe he was still in love with her.

Mary Jane squeezed her eyes shut. "So stupid." This was why she didn't bother with a social life. She was just no good at it. She should stick to teaching young children and taking care of the ailing elderly. It was the age group in between where she had the problem.

Taking it slow, since she was, as he'd said, pretty beat up, she made her way to the bed, toed off her shoes and stretched out on her back. There was always sleep.

If she were lucky, maybe she would dream about how it might have been.

SHANE'S CELL RANG. "Allen."

"We have a preliminary report from the Bureau's forensics techs."

Simon Ruhl.

"A faulty detonator," he went on, "is the only reason you two are still among the living."

Shane closed his eyes and scrubbed his free hand over his face. Damn that had been close. "Have you heard from Chicago PD as to whether they found a connection between Bailen's shooting and Torres's apparent suicide?"

"Nothing on that, but we did get the voice analysis on the call from Mary Jane's sister."

"Manufactured," Shane guessed.

"Most of the voice was a match, but the analysis indicated the dialogue had definitely been tampered with. Some portions couldn't be verified as Rebecca Brooks's voice. The statements were definitely taken from previous recordings and strung together to suit some purpose."

"Whatever went wrong," Shane surmised, "the package that was delivered to Mary Jane today was nearly a year late. The sender had explicit instructions not to send the package until some sort of confirmation that Rebecca was dead. The lab's mix-up ensured that didn't happen until about forty-eight hours ago."

"It would certainly be helpful," Ruhl suggested, "if we knew the identity of the person who mailed that package."

"Maybe," Shane offered, "maybe not. It could have been a blind job. Money paid for services rendered. For all we know, a third or even a fourth party may have had the job of sending payment. Whatever the case, now someone is scrambling to cover his ass."

"I agree," Ruhl said. "Initially, Mary Jane was probably put under surveillance. But after Rebecca had been missing for some time without any action from her sister, the unsubs thought they were in the clear and everyone was happy. But then the discovery of the glitch at the lab set this whole chain of events into motion. All because Rebecca had a backup plan and someone suspected she would have just that."

"But the remains don't belong to Rebecca Brooks," Shane reminded. "Yet another glitch."

"So we have two immediate issues to solve. Who was Rebecca Brooks afraid of?" Ruhl considered aloud. "She felt that someone was selling her out. Then there's the question of what actually happened to her. My guess is she's dead and she took the details of her secret backup plan to the grave with her. Whoever killed her couldn't ferret out what it was, but he knew all along that it would somehow involve her sister. When Mary Jane Brooks hired the Colby Agency, that someone got nervous."

"Exactly." Shane shouldered out of his jacket, moving the phone from one hand to the other. He winced at the ache in his arm. "We need a trap."

"We have the bait," Ruhl agreed. "I could send a fragment of one of the snapshots you sent me to LeMire and one to Mitchell and see who takes the bait."

Both men, both agencies, would want that evidence. The question was, which one wanted it to pursue the case against Horizon Software and which one wanted it so he could bury it…along with Rebecca Brooks?

"Sounds like a plan to me." Shane was so damned tired he certainly couldn't think of a better strategy.

"Ian and I will set this operation in motion. You and Mary Jane will be safe there. I'll give you an update first thing in the morning."

Shane had taken a long, winding, at times totally confusing, route to get here. Two other agency vehicles had run interference, ensuring they weren't followed to this location. Ruhl was right. They were safe here.

"I'll be standing by." Shane put his phone away and decided to take a shower. His body could use the relaxing heat of a long, hot shower. Then again, a cold shower might come closer to guaranteeing sleep. He couldn't get the memory of that kiss out of his head.

A kiss, short and sweet as it was, had never affected him quite that way. But he couldn't cross that line. He'd made himself a promise he wouldn't let his heart guide him again. He'd gotten so caught up in worrying about his wife and the fact that she had announced that she was leaving him for his partner, that he'd gotten himself shot. He wasn't going there again.

Not even as badly as he wanted to with this woman.

She drew him on far too many levels. Sweet, genuine and so innocent.

Any man who'd been damaged emotionally the way he had would want a woman like that. One who didn't possess the ability to tear out his heart.

But not now…not this way.

He stayed beneath the hot spray of water until it cooled and he felt halfway human again. He towel-dried his hair, scrubbed the water from his body and then slung the towel around his hips. He unwrapped the protective plastic from his arm dressing and tossed it into the trash. They had changed the dressing at the ER that evening. He was good for another day or two.

A quick check on Mary Jane and then some much-needed sleep. As safe as he was certain they were here, he couldn't let his guard down completely for anything more than snatches of shut-eye.

He'd taken two steps into the bedroom from the ensuite bath and he stalled.

Mary Jane lay snuggled beneath the covers of his bed. She didn't say a word. She didn't have to. The invitation was obvious. His body tightened instantly at the idea.

He crossed the room and sat down on the edge of the bed. "This isn't a good idea." The fact that he was naked save for the towel and that she appeared to be as well with only the sheet between them wasn't helping. The sheet molded to the sweet swell of her breasts and he had to focus hard on doing the right thing not to reach out and touch her.

"You might be right," she allowed. "But it's my idea and I don't want to wake up tomorrow wishing I'd had the courage to do what I really wanted to do. I've done that too many times already."

She touched his face, smiled so tenderly that he lost his breath.

"I could hurt you," he argued softly and without a lick of enthusiasm. "The doctor's orders stated limited physical activity."

She sank deeper into the pillows, drew him closer with that one small hand. "I trust you to be gentle."

He kissed her nose…kissed her lips. "I want to. More than you can possibly know. But I can't. Not like this." He pressed his finger to her lips when she would have argued. "But I will hold you for as long as you want me to." As hard as it would be to lie next to her and not do exactly what she wanted, he would do it.

She drew back the sheet and revealed that sweet naked body to him. He lost the towel and eased onto the mattress next to her.

He held her. Let her use his chest for a pillow. Let her touch him anyway she wanted…allowed her to explore to her heart's desire…while he died a thousand deaths. But he couldn't deny her that much.

Not for anything.

He'd let her into his already-damaged heart. He wasn't so sure how reliable it was anymore, but it was definitely hers to do with as she pleased.

Chapter Thirteen

Mary Jane awakened to the scent of warm male flesh. She inhaled deeply and relished the smell and heat of the man lying next to her. He'd been so careful how he held her last night. He'd even insisted on sleeping to her left so that he wouldn't accidentally bump her injury.

It was early and he was still asleep. One muscular arm lay draped across her chest in a protective manner. She wanted so to trace the ripples and ridges of well-defined muscle along his chest and abdomen as she had last night but didn't want to wake him. And she dreaded moving. She was sore from the impact with the asphalt, and her side ached fiercely. More painkillers would be nice, but she needed a clear head.

Shane had told her about the plan Simon Ruhl would be setting in motion to lure the traitor out into the open. Sometime during the hours they'd held each other, he'd also warned her that both he and Simon had concluded that Rebecca was dead. The voice analysis had pretty much brought Mary Jane to that same conclusion. As much as it hurt, she would like to find closure on every aspect of this nightmare. She would especially like to know what had happened to her sister.

With all that had occurred and still could, it was difficult for her to wrap her mind around any of it. She had to deal with all this one step at a time. As Shane said, stay alive first and foremost and then solve the puzzling parts of her sister's case.

If all worked out as planned, Anthony Chambers would finally get what he deserved, and whoever had betrayed her sister would get his, as well.

The idea that it could be Agent LeMire or his partner Marshal Bolton or Mitchell just seemed too incomprehensible. She had met all of these men. Each seemed quite professional and determined to bring down Chambers. Rebecca had trusted those men, and one of them had let her down.

Jason Mackey had tried to help her. From what Mary Jane knew of his background, he hadn't done a lot of right in his life. But he'd tried to do right by her sister. That was something. He'd apparently gone so far as to hire someone to die for her…only it hadn't worked out. How had the body ended up at the Colby Agency? That part just didn't make sense. Were the phone calls to the agency, calls that no one remembered taking, done specifically to tie the remains to the agency?

So much planning…all for nothing. Rebecca had been betrayed by a man whose sworn duty had been to protect her and who knew his way around anything Rebecca and her friend could have hoped to plan.

The cell phone on the bedside table rang. Shane's eyes opened. Recognition flared in those dark depths, and then he smiled.

"Morning."

Mary Jane's lips spread into an answering smile. "Good morning."

"That's my phone."

She nodded.

He rolled away from her and took the call. "Allen."

Moving in tiny increments, Mary Jane eased into a sitting position, grabbed Shane's shirt and tugged it on as she headed for the bathroom. She had to figure out how to shower without getting her dressing wet.

Voilà. A handheld shower head. Excellent. She turned on the water, shrugged off the shirt and carefully went through the cleansing ritual. By the time she'd finished and reclaimed the discarded shirt, Shane was up and dressed—except for his shirt.

"Was that an update?" She tugged on her panties and jeans. Passed him his shirt, one arm concealing her breasts even though he'd already seen them, until she could get into her bra and sweater.

"Ann is on her way here." He buttoned his shirt. "Torres's girlfriend wants to talk. She won't talk to anyone but me."

"Whoa!" Mary Jane held up both hands. She knew exactly what that meant. "You're leaving me here with Ms. Martin while you go meet Teresa?"

"That's the only way to ensure your safety."

"No way." She shook her head adamantly. "If that woman knows anything about what happened to my sister, I want to hear it firsthand."

Shane hesitated, but then, to her surprise, he didn't argue. "All right. But remember—"

"We do it your way," she finished for him.

SHANE SLOWED THE CAR AS THEY neared their rendezvous point. He should have tried harder to convince Mary Jane not to come. On the other hand, he couldn't bear the idea of allowing her out of his sight. Ann Martin was a fine investigator, but he needed to personally ensure Mary Jane was safe.

"Which one do you think it is?"

He parked in a convenience store lot and shut off the engine. "Which one what?"

"LeMire or Mitchell or one of the others?"

"I'd like to say Mitchell," he admitted. He'd like nothing better than to nail that bastard with something. But he honestly didn't believe the guy was capable of going that far over the line. But then, he'd been wrong before. "But I don't think he would do it."

"So LeMire?"

"Maybe. I don't know him or his partner that well."

"What about Bolton?"

Shane had known Bolton for years. He'd always been a by-the-book kind of guy. "Possibly. People change. Things happen that make them do things they might not otherwise do." That was an angle Ruhl was looking into. Which of those four men had suffered financial setback or any other sort of trauma in their personal or professional lives, providing motivation for crossing the line?

It would sure make Shane's life simpler if it were Mitchell. His ex might decide not to go to Denver, and then having access to Matt wouldn't be a problem.

Shane indicated a dark sedan parked farther down the street. "That's David James. He's our backup. He'll be keeping an eye out for company."

"Do you think we can trust Teresa Thomas to tell us the truth?"

Shane hated the fear in her eyes. He wished he could make that go away. "Teresa's afraid. Chances are, she's going to give us something she considers negotiable. That's usually the truth or reasonably close." He checked his watch. "Time to go."

Scanning the block with a keen eye, he waited for James to flash his headlights—the all-clear sign.

Done.

They exited the car and Shane took the most direct route to the sleaze-bag motel where Teresa Thomas was hiding out. He knocked on the door to room 114. Nearly a minute passed before the door opened.

"You're sure no one followed you?" Teresa asked

through the narrow crack she had permitted between the door and its frame. The chain latch remained in place, giving her some sense of safety.

"Positive."

She removed the chain, opened the door far enough for the two of them to come inside, then she locked and bolted it.

Teresa considered Mary Jane a moment, then she looked Shane dead in the eye. "You put me in protective custody and I'll tell you everything I know about Jason and the woman…" She glanced at Mary Jane. "Your sister."

"I need to hear the story first," Shane countered. "See how much it's worth." She might not know any more than they had already guessed. Then again, she could know everything.

She wrung her hands together in front of her. Her boyfriend's death had taken a toll. She looked as if she hadn't eaten or slept since hearing the news.

"I wanna make it clear first that I knew my Jose. No way would he kill himself. Somebody murdered him."

Most likely. "Go on," Shane said.

"Jason was head-over-heels in love with her." Teresa's tone was scarcely a notch above a snarl. "He knew his cousin was going to kill her. He wanted to help her. The problem was, he knew Anthony wouldn't stop looking for her unless he had a body." She reached for the pack of cigarettes on the table near the bed and lit one up. "He'd heard about the list, where you could buy anything, so he decided to buy someone to take her place. It wasn't like he would be murdering anybody." She waved it off. "The gal he hired had AIDS or something. She was dead, anyway."

Shane kept his sentiments on the subject to himself. He needed this woman to be cooperative. "Mackey killed this girl so he could use her body?"

Teresa shook her head. "No, it wasn't like that. She OD'd and he picked up her body at a specified time and location. It was all civilized like."

Oh, yeah. Real civilized.

"Anyway, he'd already gotten the woman's dental records and switched them for Rebecca's."

"How did her body end up in the building where Mackey died?"

"He made calls to that fancy PI agency. He'd ask a few questions, then hang up. He knew a guy in the band that had the Christmas gig that night. So he planned to take what was left of the body into the building in one of those big instrument trunks the band used. He'd dump it there like some kind of warning. *Don't rat on me or you'll end up dead.* He figured the police would connect the calls to Rebecca through him and would decide that she'd been murdered to keep her quiet and dumped publicly to warn anyone else who might know anything on Anthony. Nobody could prove Anthony did it, and

Rebecca would be off the hook—dead. Jason would disappear with her and everybody would live happily ever after. Problem was, things went wrong and Jason ended up dead." She shrugged, took a deep draw from her cigarette. "Evidently, there was some kind of mix-up and the remains didn't get found until the other day instead of last Christmas the way it was supposed to happen."

"What do you mean?" Shane asked. "He took what was left of the body to the Christmas gig?" He'd probably taken precautions to ensure the body was identified by dental records only. No way Mackey could have anticipated the building blowing up.

"He burned her...*it* first," Teresa explained. "Said it was the only way to be sure no fingerprints or anything like that was left over. He wanted her identified by the dental records. He made sure she was burned up good."

Shane resisted the impulse to shake his head at how the woman could speak of the event as if the victim had been nothing more than a disposable product. He'd make it a point to give her his thoughts on the matter once the facts were documented for legal purposes.

"As far as you know," Mary Jane jumped in to the conversation, "the night of the explosion, Rebecca was still alive?"

Shane hated to hear the renewed hope in her

voice. Each time she believed her sister might be alive, there was another letdown.

"Yeah, as far as I know. I mean—" Teresa took another puff "—I didn't, like, see her, but Jason did." She made one of those "dunno" expressions. "But after that day, she just disappeared." Teresa waved her hands. "Poof. Never heard from again. Jose said nobody could figure out what had happened to her. She had to get out of here or get dead." She eyed Shane suspiciously. "Now, do I get that protective custody or not?"

"Why didn't you tell me or the police or someone?" Mary Jane demanded, her temper flaring now that the story was told.

"And get myself killed?" Teresa tossed back. "Look what they did to Jose, and he didn't even talk!" She shook her head adamantly. "I wasn't about to let them do that to me."

Shane touched Mary Jane's arm. "Let's keep this cool." He urged her with his eyes to stay calm. This wasn't the time to send the woman running. They still needed Teresa Thomas.

Mary Jane intended to argue, he could see it in her eyes, but his cell rang and she clamped her lips together so he could take the call.

Saved by the bell. "Allen."

"Shane!"

"Sharon?" Fear erupted deep in his chest. "What's wrong?" He recognized the terror in his ex-wife's voice. Combined with the idea that she wouldn't call him unless it was bad, he had a right to be worried.

"They took Matt!" she cried. "And I can't get Derrick on his cell. He's not at the office. Oh, God!"

Ice formed in Shane's veins.

"What do you mean *they took Matt?*" All other sensation ceased. Fear, stark and vivid, claimed his entire being.

"I dropped him off at school just like always," Sharon wailed. "Then I stopped by the Starbucks. When I got home...I...I found Matt's school bag on the steps. I worried at first that he'd forgotten it, then I saw the note."

Instinct kicked in, propelling Shane from the paralysis of fear into investigator mode. "Sharon, I need you to stay calm," he urged. "Tell me what the note said."

"This is your fault," she screamed, her voice shaking. "They took him because of you! And I can't find Derrick." She lapsed into sobs. "What am I going to do?"

Shane tried to slow the pounding in his chest so he could continue to think rationally. "Sharon." He closed his eyes and struggled to hold on to his composure. "Sharon, tell me what the note said."

"You have something they need. You're to deliver it by noon today. The note says you have to go alone and that if we call the police—" she whimpered "—they'll kill Matt. You have to do some-thing, Shane! You can't let my baby get hurt! Where is Derrick?"

"Give me the address, Sharon," he pressed, his gut twisting in knots. "I need to know where I'm going."

She gave him the location between sobs.

"Stay by the phone," he ordered. "Don't talk to anyone and don't let anyone into the house." His gaze collided with Mary Jane's. "I'll find him and bring him back to you. You have my word on that."

Desolation swamped Shane as he ended the call.

Everyone who had gotten in this bastard's way had ended up dead.

No matter what he had to do, he could not let that happen to Matt. Not Matt. He was a baby. Just five years old.

Shane knew he couldn't do this alone.

He needed help.

He needed the Colby Agency.

Chapter Fourteen

Shane waited by the Ferris wheel at the Navy Pier.

The wind sliced through him like a knife.

It was 12:04.

His cell phone hadn't rung even once.

If anything happened to Matt...

He pushed the thought way. Couldn't bear to even think it.

Focus. He surveyed the die-hard shoppers and tourists rushing to and fro as if it weren't freezing out. No one approached his position. His cell phone didn't ring. Voices, conversations and laughter ran together, punctuating the grind and whir of rides and games. The smell of popcorn and cotton candy scented the chilly air, floating in off the water. To these folks it was just another day at the park.

But for Shane...his world was coming apart.

What the hell was going on with this son of a bitch? Why hadn't he called or showed?

Matt. His chest constricted. He had to be all right.

At least Mary Jane was safe. She and Ann were at the lake house. He was thankful for that.

But Matt… Anguish tore through him again. Who the hell could hurt a little kid? What kind of monster did this crap?

Simon Ruhl's voice sounded in the earpiece Shane wore. "Ian has a visual on Anthony Chambers. David just reported that Mitchell and Bolton have arrived at Sharon's place."

Damn it. "Sharon won't be able to keep this from them," Shane muttered. If Mitchell or Bolton did anything to screw this up…

"I've asked David to intercede if necessary."

That should go over like a lead balloon. Shane could think of at least two laws that tactic would break. "Copy that." As long as Matt was okay when this was said and done, nothing else mattered.

One thing was certain—if Mitchell and Bolton were with Sharon, that basically ruled out either of them as suspects.

Unless someone was doing the dirty work for them.

No way. This was something that would be handled personally. It was too important. No one in their right mind, except maybe Anthony Chambers, would risk allowing just anyone to take care of this sensitive matter.

"What about LeMire?" Shane asked as he studied the crowd moving around him as if he didn't even exist. Ian's wife, Nicole, had LeMire and his partner, Farmer, under surveillance. Nicole was former FBI; she knew how these guys operated.

Where the hell was his contact? Shane glanced at his watch. This wasn't right.

"LeMire hasn't made a move," Ruhl advised. "He and Farmer are having lunch. Nicole is two tables away, munching on shrimp cocktail."

This didn't make sense. Rebecca Brooks had been so sure it was one of them…that someone assigned to her case was dirty. If it wasn't Mitchell or Bolton, or LeMire or Farmer, then that left no one but Chambers. Bailen was dead.

Who the hell was doing this?

There was nothing Shane could do but hold his position…and pray.

Ten, then twenty minutes passed and nothing.

No contact whatsoever.

Nothing.

Either he'd been given the wrong information or—

"Allen, we have a problem."

The hair on the back of Shane's neck bristled. "What've you got?"

"We have a distress signal from Martin. She and Ms. Brooks have left the lake house."

The blood drained into Shane's boots. The realization of what those words meant roared through him. "We've been had. This was a decoy." Fury blasted through him, sending the blood barreling through his veins once more. He headed for the closest exit. Not only was Matt in danger, but now Mary Jane was, as well.

Shane had screwed up. He should have seen this coming.

"Stay put, Allen," Ruhl ordered. "I repeat, hold your position. Until we have confirmation on the nature of the problem with Martin you stay right where you are."

Was he kidding?

Before Shane could argue, Ruhl said, "We can't take the risk, man. We have to play this hand the way it was dealt."

Desperation sucked the fury out of Shane's bones. Ruhl was right.

He had no choice but to stay right here…and wait. Ann and Mary Jane were adults…Matt was a child. The risk was too great.

"Stand by," Ruhl said, then paused. "I just received word from Ian that Chambers is on the move."

That was it. "I can't hold this position," Shane argued. Something was going down, and it sure as hell wasn't doing it *here.*

"Ian is on this, Allen," Ruhl countered. "You have your orders. You're going to have to trust me on this."

Shane hadn't trusted anyone on this level— deeply personal—in more than a year. He wasn't sure he could now…

"WE CAN'T DO THIS WITHOUT notifying Simon or Ian."

Mary Jane ignored Ann's protests and kept

driving toward the rendezvous location she had been given. They had to hurry. Time was running out.

Rebecca had called.

There was no question. It was Rebecca. Not some recording. Not someone pretending. No matter what the voice analysis had said, Mary Jane knew. They had to reach that cabin. It was well outside Chicago, close to Crystal Lake. She didn't know the area that well, but she knew how to read road signs. Two turns. That was all it would take once they left the interstate.

"This is a mistake," Ann tacked on for emphasis.

"If that child dies," Mary Jane argued with a pointed glance in the other woman's direction, "because we failed to follow instructions, how do you plan to live with that?" Every time her mind replayed that little boy's voice calling for Shane, an ache pierced her straight through the heart. The man holding Rebecca had put him on the line, too. He had them both, Rebecca and Matt.

Mary Jane couldn't worry about how any of this was possible right now or why it was happening. She just had to do what she had to do. No questions, no hesitation. *Just do it.*

When the call had first come, Ann had refused to allow Mary Jane to go. Mary Jane had called her bluff. "Shoot me then," she'd said. Ann hadn't argued the point any further.

After leaving the Colby safe house, their first

stop had been the bank. Mary Jane had taken the CD
from the safety deposit box. The one Shane was
using was a fake made with the files he'd snapped
digital images of with his cell phone. Somehow this
scumbag had known Shane would try to avoid
giving him the original CD, and he wanted the
original. Or so he had said. Rebecca had passed
along his instructions, fear and desperation in her
trembling voice. That part didn't make sense to
Mary Jane, but then what was sensible about kid-
napping and murder?

"This isn't about the CD," Ann warned. "You
have to know it isn't. We could have made a thousand
copies of those documents, any one of which would
stand up in court every bit as well as the original. This
is about getting you to a remote location."

Mary Jane wasn't so naïve that she didn't see
that. But what choice did she have? It was either go
or risk that little boy's life. And her sister's.

Rebecca was alive.

Mary Jane's heart reacted to another surge of
adrenaline. She wasn't sure she would really believe
it until she saw Rebecca with her own eyes, but she
couldn't deny the voice…the call.

Mary Jane parked twenty yards or so from their
final turn. They were here, finally.

Ann shifted in her seat to look directly at Mary
Jane. "We should wait for backup. I sent a distress
signal. They know where we are. One of my col-

leagues will be close behind us. We could have plenty of support within minutes."

Uncertainty crowded into Mary Jane's throat as she surveyed the long desolate road behind them. She wasn't sure. But she should have anticipated Ann would do something like that. Protecting Mary Jane was her job. As much as she appreciated that, she wasn't sure this could wait.

"What if they don't get here in time?" Now she was hesitating. Oh, God. What should she do? She was just a school teacher. She wasn't trained for this kind of thing, but she had her orders. *"Come quickly. Don't wait! We need you,"* Rebecca had urged. *"He's going to kill us if you don't hurry!"*

Mary Jane's cell rang, causing her heart to practically stop. She stared at the display, then at Ann. "It's her." Mary Jane moistened her lips. "Hello."

"Are you here?"

Rebecca.

Mary Jane swallowed back the emotion. "Almost."

"Oh, MJ, you have to hurry." She lowered her voice to a barely discernible whisper. "He's going to kill us both. Please hurry. I don't know—"

The call ended.

Mary Jane dropped her phone and reached for the door handle.

"Wait," Ann urged as she grabbed Mary Jane's arm. "If sending Allen to the Navy Pier was a decoy, then this is the real thing, Mary Jane. We have to go in strategically, not emotionally. Let me go first. I want you to stay behind me at all times."

She sounded like Shane. Mary Jane managed a stiff nod. Were all Colby Agency investigators trained to act as human shields to protect their clients, paying or not? Was Mary Jane's decision to act on Rebecca's call about to get this woman killed?

It was too late for second thoughts now.

Too terrified to do anything but follow, Mary Jane stayed close behind Ann. They made their way through the trees and underbrush along the narrow dirt road that led from the main highway to where a cabin stood well hidden from view.

Anthony Chambers's cabin, according to the information Rebecca had provided.

Mary Jane didn't know what kind of car he drove, but she would bet that the luxury SUV stationed next to the cabin was his.

"If we can get close enough on this side," Ann said quietly as she pointed to the east end of the cabin, "we may be able to get a look inside or be able to hear conversation without being spotted. We need to ascertain how many we're up against."

There was no sign of any other vehicles in the area. Just the one SUV. But that didn't mean there weren't a dozen of Chambers's men in there.

Mary Jane nodded. "Let's try." Her side burned

like fire and she was sore as all get-out, but she kept pace with Ann's swift movements.

The cold November air stung Mary Jane's face, made her eyes water. Her sister was in that cabin. Alive. Her heart thudded hard. Where had Rebecca been all this time? Why hadn't she tried to contact Mary Jane before now?

Ann paused to survey the clearing before breaking from the cover of the trees. They reached the end of the cabin and listened. Voices. Too muffled to comprehend but there was no question that the discussion inside was a full-scale argument or debate.

Then one voice, female, sounded louder than the other.

"Rebecca." Mary Jane's gaze collided with Ann's. "She's here. I have to go in there now. She and Matt—"

"Wait," Ann urged in a harsh whisper. "Let me go first. We have to maintain the element of surprise. It's the only thing we have going for us right now."

Mary Jane started to argue, but movement at the rear corner of the house snapped her gaze in that direction. Ann's weapon leveled.

Ian Michaels.

Mary Jane's heart slid back down into her chest and started to beat once more. Ann lowered the bead she had on Ian. He did the same.

"I followed Chambers here," he explained.

Chambers was in there with Matt…with Rebecca. Fear filled Mary Jane's chest with pure ice.

"I have to get in there," she said, dividing her attention between the two Colby Agency investigators. Didn't they get it? She couldn't keep putting this off, or someone was going to die.

"You're right," Ian agreed.

"What?" Ann stared at him as if he'd lost his mind. "If she goes in there—"

"There's only one way to do this," Ian cut her off. "We need Chambers distracted while we get into place to take control of the situation."

"What if he has one or more of his buddies in there?" Ann argued. "I don't like this."

"He came alone," Ian advised.

That news stunned Mary Jane almost as much as it did Ann. "But there is someone else in there," Mary Jane reminded them. "Whoever held my sister and Matt hostage until Chambers got here. That person is in there."

"We can handle those odds," Ian said without hesitation. "But we have to use the right strategy to ensure that no one gets hurt."

Ann didn't argue with her superior, but she was obviously skeptical. Mary Jane just wanted this over.

About three minutes later, she made her way through the trees, taking the path she and Ann had used previously to the bend in the dirt road. Then she headed back toward the cabin to make it look as if she had just come from the road. If anyone was watching that was, hopefully, what they would think.

Mary Jane climbed the steps, her heart thumping so hard she was certain it would fail anytime, and crossed the porch. She took a breath, raised her fist and banged on the door.

The door swung open and Anthony Chambers stared at her. She, conversely, stared at the gun in his hand.

He grabbed her by the lapel of her jacket and yanked her inside. Pain shot through her side, making her stomach churn dangerously. She was pretty sure he wouldn't be too happy if she barfed on him. She'd been doing a lot of that lately.

"Give him the CD," Rebecca cried.

That was when the world stopped for Mary Jane.

She could only stare at her sister. Her strawberry-blond hair was shorter…but otherwise she looked exactly the same. Blue eyes round with fear, pale skin flushed with the same.

Rebecca was alive. She clutched a little boy in her arms. Matt. Shane's stepson.

"I should have killed you when I had the chance," Chambers threatened, his furious gaze burning up the air between him and Rebecca.

Mary Jane experienced a moment of panic. "The CD," she said to Chambers. "It's in my coat pocket." Please let this distract his fury away from Rebecca long enough for Ian and Ann to get in place.

Chambers glowered at Mary Jane. "What the hell are you talking about?"

"Don't listen to him," Rebecca cried. "Just give him the CD!"

Matt wailed in fear.

Mary Jane's heart shattered. The child was scared to death. Chambers was still glowering at her as if he was startled or confused.

"He's up to something," Rebecca warned, tears flowing down her cheeks. Her eyes were puffy from hours of crying. Her voice was hoarse from the pleading or shouting or both.

But where was the other man? The one who had been holding Rebecca and Matt here until Chambers arrived.

Chambers shoved Mary Jane toward her sister. Pain knifed through her and she had to breathe long and deeply through her nose to ride out the agony. She had to focus, couldn't let him see the weakness.

"You waited all this time," Chambers said savagely, "to try and finish the job. Well, it's not going to work. It didn't work before and it won't work now. You can't possibly believe you're smarter than me!"

This was Mary Jane's chance. She stepped in front of Rebecca and Matt. It took every ounce of courage she possessed to look into the man's eye and speak calmly. "You should put the gun down, Mr. Chambers."

He stared at Mary Jane, the fury contorting his

face turning to confusion again. "What the hell are you doing?"

She reached into her pocket, hesitated when the business end of his gun shifted fully on her. "I have the CD." She withdrew the CD and he visibly relaxed as if he'd feared she was carrying a weapon. "This is what you want. Take it and go. No one else needs to die."

If she could convince him to leave, Ann and Ian would nail him outside. Mary Jane could keep Rebecca and Matt safe in here. It could work.

"This is insane!" The gun in his hand shook.

That was the moment when Mary Jane understood that something was terribly wrong. All those months ago, she had watched a cool, seemingly unaffected man in the news as he had denied the accusations against him. She had watched him walk away from all charges since the FBI's key witness had disappeared. She had hated him, had been certain he had done something to harm her sister. But now…here, there was something in the man's eyes…in his expression that didn't fit.

"Watch out, Mary Jane!"

A body slammed into Mary Jane's back, forcing her forward. What the…?

The weapon in Chambers's hand leveled on her once more.

The door burst open.

"Drop your weapon, Chambers!"

Ian Michaels stood in the open doorway. He had a bead on the man.

"Do as he says, Chambers." Ann Martin's voice came from somewhere behind Mary Jane, but she didn't dare turn around to look.

That cornered-animal look seized Chambers's face.

Mary Jane knew he was going to act.

"Drop it," Ian repeated, "or I will shoot you where you stand."

Where was the other man?

As much as she wanted to see for herself, Mary Jane couldn't risk taking her eyes off Chambers, but she sensed that there was no one behind her except Rebecca, Matt and Ann. Otherwise Ann would have been ordering around the other guy. But then, who had barreled into her?

Mary Jane spotted the panic in Chambers's eyes a split second before he made his decision.

She had to do something.

"Wait!" she shouted.

The weapon Chambers would have swung in Ian's direction held steady on her.

"Something's wrong," she announced to all listening, uncertainty and fear twisting inside her. "This is…not right."

"You're damned right there's something wrong," Chambers snapped. "That crazy sister of yours—"

"Oh, God, Mary Jane!" Rebecca wailed.

"Don't you see he's playing you? Someone needs to stop him!"

Mary Jane didn't take her eyes off the man. With every fiber of her being she knew…she knew her sister was *lying*.

"You," Chambers said to her, "come with me!"

"Stay right where you are, Ms. Brooks," Ian ordered.

"Don't move, Mary Jane," Ann cautioned.

"MJ? What're you doing?" Rebecca shrieked. "He'll kill you!"

This had to end. Mary Jane stepped forward, allowed Chambers to drag her against his chest with one muscled arm wrapped around her throat. He shoved the gun against her head. "Back off," he shouted to the room at large. "I'll let her go as soon as I'm back in the city as long as nobody tries to follow me."

Ian mimicked every step Chambers made toward the door, refused to lower his weapon but he made no move of aggression. Mary Jane wished he would just let them go. Then Matt would be safe… Rebecca would be safe.

Chambers dragged Mary Jane out onto the porch. He'd backed all the way to the steps without taking his eyes off Ian when another voice caused him to stall.

"Let her go, Chambers, or I will put a bullet in your brain. You have until three. One…"

Shane. Mary Jane's pulse leaped. He was here. Thank God.

"Two," Shane warned.

"No way!" Chambers roared. "I know what you'll do if I let her go." His hold on Mary Jane tightened. "You'll kill me. You people have been looking for an excuse for more than a year. No way am I giving you the opportunity. If I die, she dies."

Mary Jane clutched at his arm when his hold tightened to the point of cutting off her airway. She struggled to get a breath.

"Three!"

The bullet exploding from the weapon was deafening.

Chambers's weapon flew out of his hand. He stumbled backward. Mary Jane collapsed onto her knees on the porch and gasped for air. Her gaze landed on Chambers, expecting to find his head blown apart. Instead, the man wailed like a banshee, blood spurting from his right hand.

"Don't move," Shane warned as he crouched down to check the man's injury.

Mary Jane wasn't sure exactly what had happened, but she was very glad that it had. Three more Colby Agency investigators, Simon Ruhl, David James and a man she hadn't met before, rushed toward the porch. The sound of a siren in the distance allowed her to draw in a deep breath for the first time in days.

Rebecca rushed out onto the porch. Ann Martin was right behind her with the boy in her arms.

"He's still alive?" Rebecca shouted as her attention fell on Chambers. "Why didn't you shoot him?" She stumbled back several steps. "I'll never be free until he's dead!"

Mary Jane pushed to her feet and went to her sister. She held her in an attempt to comfort her. Rebecca resisted at first, then she surrendered, collapsing against Mary Jane's shoulder as her body convulsed with sobs.

Ian took over for Shane so that he could take Matt, who was calling his name. Tears welled in Mary Jane's eyes. Thank God. Matt was safe. And no one else had died.

Her attention settled back on the woman in her arms. Wherever Rebecca had been hiding for the past year, whatever had happened before she disappeared, the woman hanging on to Mary Jane right now was not the sister she had known as a child.

Rebecca Brooks was alive…but Mary Jane's sister was dead.

MARY JANE SAT AT HER KITCHEN table and ate a bowl of cereal as she watched the fish dart around in the tank sitting on her counter. Two weeks had passed, and she still felt exhausted from all that had happened.

Anthony Chambers had not facilitated the sale of secrets to enemies of the state.

Rebecca had. With the help of Special Agent LeMire.

The two had made millions and then tried to pin the whole thing on Anthony Chambers. Mary Jane was certain the complicated ruse that had played out would make a fantastic mystery novel. She was also certain that no one would ever know all the details of what had really happened.

Except for the part where her own flesh and blood was one of the bad guys.

Rebecca and LeMire had had it all planned out and then something had gone wrong. The lab had made a mistake. They'd had no choice but to wait it out. Anything either of them might have done would have triggered suspicion. Once the remains were confirmed as Rebecca's, the plan was set in motion and the race was on to get Anthony Chambers out of the way. He was supposed to end up dead. Then Rebecca and LeMire could go on with their lives and their millions and no one would have been the wiser.

The phone calls. The package. The whole elaborate hoax had been planned and executed, at least in part, by her sister. Whoever had gotten in the way had died. Like Detective Bailen. He had started asking too many pointed questions of LeMire. Jose Torres had been the only other person besides LeMire who had known Rebecca was still alive.

He'd kept his mouth shut, played his part and still they had killed him just to tie up loose ends.

Rebecca was a murderer and a traitor. She had convinced LeMire to align with her when he started investigating Chambers. Rebecca had known she would need an ally.

Mary Jane wasn't sure she would ever get over that hurt. It still seemed impossible. Ambition had turned to greed...greed had evolved into something uglier.

She had no family left...except for Shane. She smiled as he shuffled into the kitchen, his lounge pants riding low on his lean hips. His gorgeous chest bare.

"You didn't eat all the cereal, did you?" He grabbed the box and shook it.

God, she loved looking at him. The warmth that filled her at his mere presence chased away the chill that thoughts of her sister had elicited. "There might be enough left for you," Mary Jane teased. She suddenly wished she had pulled on something a little sexier than this pink flannel gown this morning.

He poured a bowlful of the crispy flakes and nuts. "I've been thinking," he said. "We should take a vacation. Get away for a while. It would be good for both of us."

"What about Matt and Christmas?" Sharon had decided that Shane deserved visitation rights. She and Derrick Mitchell would be moving to Denver as planned, but with an open invitation for Shane to visit anytime.

Shane dropped into the chair across the table from Mary Jane. "Okay, so after Christmas." He poured milk over his cereal. "Someplace warm."

He'd asked her to marry him already, but she'd been putting off giving him an answer. They had needed time to get to know each other…for the dust to settle. *They* actually meaning *she*. With all that had happened, she'd needed time to adjust…to think.

"Okay," she agreed.

He hesitated, the spoon halfway to his sexy mouth. "You're agreeing to a vacation with me?"

She smiled. "That and I'm agreeing to your earlier question."

Those dark eyes melted with emotion. "You'll marry me?"

She nodded. "Yes. Someplace warm right after Christmas."

He dropped his spoon, stood, pushed his bowl aside and leaned across the table so that he could brush his lips across hers. "It's about time," he murmured.

He kissed her for real, and she forgot all about traitors and murderers and her treacherous sister. *This* was about her. Mary Jane Brooks. From this day forward, her life was going to be very different.

Her fingers dove into Shane's silky hair. Oh, yes. She had lots of catching up to do.

Starting right now.

Two days later...
Colby Agency

VICTORIA COLBY-CAMP stood by her beloved window and watched the pedestrians rush to work. It was early and it was a beautiful morning, even so close to Thanksgiving. She lifted her coffee mug to her lips. All was as it should be. The agency was fully back on its feet after losing its home of more than two decades. Her outstanding staff was settled in and performing in the same superior manner clients had come to expect from the best of the best. Not a single glitch anywhere to be found. The world was as it should be. And, any day now she would be a grandmother for the second time. Her son, Jim, had launched his own firm, the Equalizers, and business had increased to the point that he would need to hire a couple more new associates. Though his decision was not the one Victoria expected, she respected his determination and ambition. Just a few months ago Jim had begun taking his first university classes toward a law degree. He and his young family were truly on their way to a bright future.

After twenty-five years of pain and anguish Victoria's life was finally back on track. One way or another, one case at a time, she intended to see that it stayed that way. Someday she would tell Colby Agency stories to her grandchildren. Maybe even write her biography. But, for now, she was perfectly happy being Victoria Colby-Camp.

The intercom on her desk buzzed and she smiled. Time to get to work. She moved to her desk and pressed the necessary button. "Yes?"

Mildred, her long-time friend and personal assistant, quickly explained that a potential client had arrived. This client didn't have an appointment, but she was desperate.

"Send her in," Victoria announced, then looked up as the door to her office opened. "Welcome to the Colby Agency."

The young woman looked uncertain, but didn't hesitate to stride right up to Victoria's desk and offer her hand in greeting. "I hope you can help me," she implored, emotion welling in her eyes. "I'm at the end of my rope."

Victoria indicated one of the chairs stationed in front of her desk. "Don't worry, you've come to the right place."

* * * * *

SPECIAL EDITION®

LIFE, LOVE AND FAMILY

*These contemporary romances will strike
a chord with you as heroines juggle life and
relationships on their way to true love.*

New York Times *bestselling author
Linda Lael Miller brings you a
BRAND-NEW contemporary story
featuring her fan-favorite McKettrick family.*

Meg McKettrick is surprised to be reunited
with her high school flame, Brad O'Ballivan.
After enjoying a career as a country-and-
western singer, Brad aches for a home and
family…and seeing Meg again makes him
realize he still loves her. But their pride
manages to interfere with love…until an unexpected matchmaker gets involved.

Turn the page for a sneak preview of
THE McKETTRICK WAY
by Linda Lael Miller
On sale November 20,
wherever books are sold.

Brad shoved the truck into gear and drove to the bottom of the hill, where the road forked. Turn left, and he'd be home in five minutes. Turn right, and he was headed for Indian Rock.

He had no damn business going to Indian Rock.

He had nothing to say to Meg McKettrick, and if he never set eyes on the woman again, it would be two weeks too soon.

He turned right.

He couldn't have said why.

He just drove straight to the Dixie Dog Drive-In.

Back in the day, he and Meg used to meet at the Dixie Dog, by tacit agreement, when either of them had been away. It had been some kind of universe thing, purely intuitive.

Passing familiar landmarks, Brad told himself he ought to turn around. The old days were gone. Things had ended badly between him and Meg anyhow, and she wasn't going to be at the Dixie Dog.

He kept driving.

He rounded a bend, and there was the Dixie Dog. Its big neon sign, a giant hot dog, was all lit up and going through its corny sequence—first it was covered in red squiggles of light, meant to suggest ketchup, and then yellow, for mustard.

Brad pulled into one of the slots next to a speaker, rolled down the truck window and ordered.

A girl roller-skated out with the order about five minutes later.

When she wheeled up to the driver's window, smiling, her eyes went wide with recognition, and she dropped the tray with a clatter.

Silently Brad swore. Damn if he hadn't forgotten he was a famous country singer.

The girl, a skinny thing wearing too much eye makeup, immediately started to cry. "I'm sorry!" she sobbed, squatting to gather up the mess.

"It's okay," Brad answered quietly, leaning to look down at her, catching a glimpse of her plastic name tag. "It's okay, Mandy. No harm done."

"I'll get you another dog and a shake right away, Mr. O'Ballivan!"

"Mandy?"

She stared up at him pitifully, sniffling. Thanks to the copious tears, most of the goop on her eyes had slid south. "Yes?"

"When you go back inside, could you not mention seeing me?"

"But you're Brad O'Ballivan!"

"Yeah," he answered, suppressing a sigh. "I know."

She rolled a little closer. "You wouldn't happen to have a picture you could autograph for me, would you?"

"Not with me," Brad answered.

"You could sign this napkin, though," Mandy said. "It's only got a little chocolate on the corner."

Brad took the paper napkin and her order pen, and scrawled his name. Handed both items back through the window.

She turned and whizzed back toward the side entrance to the Dixie Dog.

Brad waited, marveling that he hadn't considered incidents like this one before he'd decided to come back home. In retrospect, it seemed shortsighted, to say the least, but the truth was, he'd expected to be—Brad O'Ballivan.

Presently Mandy skated back out again, and this time she managed to hold on to the tray.

"I didn't tell a soul!" she whispered. "But Heather and Darlene *both* asked me why my mascara was all smeared." Efficiently she hooked the tray on to the bottom edge of the window.

Brad extended payment, but Mandy shook her head.

"The boss said it's on the house, since I dumped your first order on the ground."

He smiled. "Okay, then. Thanks."

Mandy retreated, and Brad was just reaching for the food when a bright red Blazer whipped into the space beside his. The driver's door sprang open, crashing into the metal speaker, and somebody got out in a hurry.

Something quickened inside Brad.

And in the next moment Meg McKettrick was standing practically on his running board, her blue eyes blazing.

Brad grinned. "I guess you're not over me after all," he said.

REQUEST YOUR FREE BOOKS!

2 FREE NOVELS PLUS 2 FREE GIFTS!

◆ HARLEQUIN®

INTRIGUE®

Breathtaking Romantic Suspense

YES! Please send me 2 FREE Harlequin Intrigue® novels and my 2 FREE gifts. After receiving them, if I don't wish to receive any more books, I can return the shipping statement marked "cancel." If I don't cancel, I will receive 6 brand-new novels every month and be billed just $4.24 per book in the U.S., or $4.99 per book in Canada, plus 25¢ shipping and handling per book and applicable taxes, if any*. That's a savings of close to 15% off the cover price! I understand that accepting the 2 free books and gifts places me under no obligation to buy anything. I can always return a shipment and cancel at any time. Even if I never buy another book from Harlequin, the two free books and gifts are mine to keep forever.

182 HDN EEZ7   382 HDN EEZK

Name	(PLEASE PRINT)	
Address		Apt. #
City	State/Prov.	Zip/Postal Code

Signature (if under 18, a parent or guardian must sign)

Mail to the **Harlequin Reader Service®**:
IN U.S.A.: P.O. Box 1867, Buffalo, NY 14240-1867
IN CANADA: P.O. Box 609, Fort Erie, Ontario L2A 5X3

Not valid to current Harlequin Intrigue subscribers.

Want to try two free books from another line?
Call 1-800-873-8635 or visit www.morefreebooks.com.

* Terms and prices subject to change without notice. NY residents add applicable sales tax. Canadian residents will be charged applicable provincial taxes and GST. This offer is limited to one order per household. All orders subject to approval. Credit or debit balances in a customer's account(s) may be offset by any other outstanding balance owed by or to the customer. Please allow 4 to 6 weeks for delivery.

Your Privacy: Harlequin is committed to protecting your privacy. Our Privacy Policy is available online at www.eHarlequin.com or upon request from the Reader Service. From time to time we make our lists of customers available to reputable firms who may have a product or service of interest to you. If you would prefer we not share your name and address, please check here. ☐

HI07

Inside ROMANCE

Stay up-to-date on all your
romance reading news!

Inside Romance is a FREE quarterly newsletter
highlighting our upcoming series releases
and promotions.

Visit
www.eHarlequin.com/InsideRomance
to sign up to receive our complimentary newsletter today!

IRNI I07

Get ready to meet

THREE WISE WOMEN

with stories by

DONNA BIRDSELL,
LISA CHILDS

and

SUSAN CROSBY.

Don't miss these three unforgettable stories
about modern-day women and the love
and new lives they find on Christmas.

Look for *Three Wise Women*
Available December wherever you buy books.

ATHENA FORCE

Heart-pounding romance and thrilling adventure.

She's their ace in the hole.

Posing as a glamorous high roller, Bethany James, a professional gambler and sometimes government agent, uncovers a mob boss's deadly secrets...and the ugly sins from his past. But when a daredevil with a tantalizing drawl calls her bluff, the stakes—and her heart rate—become much, much higher. Beth can't help but wonder: Have the cards been finally stacked against her?

ATHENA FORCE

Will the women of Athena unravel Arachne's powerful web of blackmail and death...or succumb to their enemies' deadly secrets?

Look for

STACKED DECK
by *Terry Watkins.*

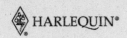

HARLEQUIN®

INTRIGUE®

COMING NEXT MONTH

#1029 UP IN FLAMES by Rita Herron
Nighthawk Island
Detective Bradford Walsh believed only in hard facts. But after saving
Rosanna Redhill from a firebug setting Savannah ablaze, was he being
led somewhere even more combustible?

#1030 CLASSIFIED CHRISTMAS by B.J. Daniels
Whitehorse, Montana
Cade Jackson had loved Texas girls before, and it led to nothing but
trouble. But after new girl in town Andi Blake is kidnapped, it was up
to the Montana cowboy to recover a missing three million dollars
before the Christmas deadline.

#1031 WOLF MOON by Patricia Rosemoor
The McKenna Legacy
After Rhys Lindgren tried to chase Alieen McKenna back to the big
city, she suspected he wasn't all human...but that didn't stop her from
reentering the wilderness to break all the boundaries.

#1032 TELLING SECRETS by Tracy Montoya
Search-and-rescue tracker Alex Gray didn't believe Sophie Brennan's
predictions—until they began coming true. But would he heed
her warnings when his path took them past the Renegade Ridge
Mountains to find his missing father?

#1033 ALASKAN FANTASY by Elle James
Would Sam Russell and Kat Sikes outrace a killer on the frozen
Alaskan trail, only to find cold comfort in each other?

#1034 THE STRANGER AND I by Carol Ericson
Covert operative Justin Vidal was a man on the edge until Lila Monroe
pulled him back. But now her fate rested in the hands of a reckless
stranger caught in a web of lethal spies.

HICNM1107